The Phantom Fiddler

&

Other Notable Tales

Joe McHugh

Calling Crane Publishing
www.callingcrane.com

© 2014 Joe McHugh

Cover Design: Paula McHugh

Chapter Illustration: Paula McHugh

Front Cover: Photograph taken in 1914 near Asheville, NC, by William A. Barnhill. The fiddler is believed to be Quill Rose.

Printed in the United States of America

This book is dedicated to all the fiddlers,
past and present, who love and carry forward
this venerable tradition.

And I never started to plow in my life
That some one did not stop in the road
And take me away to a dance or picnic.
I ended up with forty acres;
I ended up with a broken fiddle—
And a broken laugh, and a thousand memories,
And not a single regret.

~ from "Fiddler Jones" by Edgar Lee Masters

Contents

THE
PHANTOM
FIDDLER

You have heard it said that people do not change. Well, don't you believe it. They *do* change, and sometimes for the better. It doesn't happen often, I'll grant you that, but take Otto Grumgenhoff, for instance. A bachelor by temperament and choice, he emigrated from Germany to the United States in 1886 after deserting the Prussian Army. He wasn't the only one stealing across a border at night or smuggling himself onto a ship. Many young men came to America to avoid military service. You could say, and rightfully so, that our country was settled by a bunch of draft dodgers.

Now as fate would have it, Grumgenhoff settled in Pittsburgh, where he got a job in a tannery on the north side of the city. For generations his father's family in Germany had been in the leather business, so Grumgenhoff knew the trade, and in time the owners made him a foreman.

Every evening after returning to his small room at the boarding house, he would sit on the bed and count his earnings. He never spent money on drink or paid for a meal at a restaurant. And God forbid he should buy a ticket to a dance or take in a minstrel show. You see Grumgenhoff had a dream. He wanted above all things to own and operate his own hotel like the hotels his mother's brothers owned in Frankfurt and Cologne. But that meant saving every cent he could lay his hands on. Never a churchgoer, he even took up usury, having no scruples in that direction. Whenever a German immigrant was hard pressed for money and couldn't get a loan from a bank, Grumgenhoff would lend him the dough, provided the man was desperate enough to agree to pay three times the interest the bank charged.

In this way, Grumgenhoff managed in the span of ten years to save up enough to buy his hotel. Only he couldn't afford a city hotel, so he cast about until he found one for sale high up in the mountains of West Virginia. The hotel was called the Mountain Laurel.

Now, why a man like Grumgenhoff wanted to buy a hotel in the first place is a mystery because there never was a person less suited to the role of innkeeper. Heavy-set, with florid features and lamb chop sideburns, and a starched apron draped like a revival tent over his prodigious girth, the German bossed his guests about with the stiff irritability of a schoolmaster suffering from piles. He never laughed at a joke and you would as soon get a friendly word out of him about the weather, the price of coal, or how the governor's son was found shot dead in a cathouse in Huntington as you would get beer out of a Salvation Army tambourine. Thus, you might conclude that a person with that kind of temperament would fail in the hotel business. The widow Strale predicted as much after she sold the Mountain Laurel to Grumgenhoff. That was after her husband Gideon died of tuberculosis of the bone.

"That cranky German must eat a fistful of tacks every morning for breakfast," she told Willis Plumbly, the local mail carrier, "he's so gruff and short with people. Now you take Gid, God rest his soul, he knew how to jolly up the guests. He'd ask after their wives and children and shake his head and frown if they complained that business wasn't so good. You hear what I'm saying? Grumgenhoff doesn't give a fig what people do or say so long as they behave themselves and pay their bill. I doubt a year will pass before he sells up and moves on."

But Grumgenhoff didn't sell up and move on. Instead, each year he watched his profits grow, if only modestly. And why is that? Because the Mountain Laurel was the only hotel for miles around. Built the year the Civil War ended, the hotel straddled a pass in the mountains that separated the capital city of Charleston from the coal mining towns in the southern part of the state. A rambling, two-story, wood-framed structure with a covered porch facing the road, the Mountain Laurel provided the weary wagoners, drovers, and peddlers who passed that way bug-free beds and affordable meals.

All through the late spring, summer, and fall the Mountain Laurel bustled with activity. Many a night guests were forced to share their beds with fellow sojourners, the hotel was that crowded. In winter, however, snow closed the pass and few travelers ventured that way. In anticipation of this, Grumgenhoff would swing the heavy window shutters closed and bolt them from the inside. He would then drop a beam across the kitchen door and lock the front door with a key before driving his trap down the mountain to Charleston where he caught the train that took him first to Baltimore and then to Georgia. That is where his spinster sister lived and he would stay with her through the winter months and not return to the Mountain Laurel until the Ides of March. Then he would fling the shutters open, haul the linens outside to air them, replace any broken shingles, uncover the well, and drive the squirrels from the attic. This took him three days and on the fourth, March 19th, he opened for business.

Year after year it was the same routine, the hotel slumbering like a bear through the winter months while its owner sat in his sister's parlor smoking cigars, drinking peppermint schnapps, and expecting the poor woman to wait on him hand and foot.

The year was 1902 and a fraternal organization in Charleston decided to host a fiddle contest to raise money for the wives and children of coal miners who had died in accidents. The event committee included some of the leading citizens of the city and they were preparing to go whole hog for the big day.

The first thing they did was rent the Odd Fellows Hall and set the date for the contest for the first Saturday in December. They then printed up large, full-color posters and ran advertisements in newspapers throughout West Virginia, as well as three neighboring states. The prize for first place, they trumpeted, was fifty dollars, with the second place winner pocketing half that amount. The third place winner would receive an eighteen-pound smoked ham. Each winner would also receive a colored silk ribbon that he could tie to the scroll of his fiddle for showing off when he got back home.

The head judge for the contest was none other than the legendary fiddler Pop Moran. He was assisted by Bernie

McQuire, choir director at Saint Mark's Methodist Church, and Angelo Nocida, known throughout the city as the "singing cobbler."

At last the night for the big contest arrived and the Odd Fellows Hall was decked out in patriotic bunting and Christmas wreaths. Gaslights mounted along the walls illuminated the hall and every seat was occupied, with several dozen more folks standing shoulder to shoulder along the back wall. Shrouds of tobacco smoke hung in the air and coins clinked as moonshine dealers slipped fruit jars from under their coats into the hands of thirsty customers.

When all was in readiness, the judges filed into the hall and took up their post at a table on the floor in front of the stage. Pop Moran took the middle seat, his hair so white that from the back he looked like a fence post after a winter storm.

The crowd was in high spirits. The racket of their excited conversation, laughter, and hearty salutations filled the hall.

Then Harlen Griffin, the mayor, who had agreed to serve as master of ceremonies, stepped out onto the stage, and the crowd quieted down.

"Are we here to have a good time tonight?" the mayor boomed in his familiar vote-for-me baritone.

He was answered with hoots and hollers and thunderous applause. Feuds were forgotten and worry left at home by the hearthside because tonight everyone was intent on having fun and hearing some top-notch fiddle music.

"I realize you have already shelled out for a ticket to this wonderful event, but let me remind you that we are raising money for a worthy cause. Consider the noble, hardworking miner who goes underground every day to provide us with the coal we need to run our factories and heat our homes.

But then there is a roof fall or a gas explosion and the unfortunate man loses his life. Who, I ask you, will look after his wife and little ones? Well, ladies and gentlemen, that is why we are here tonight, and if my assistants will now come forward, see if you can give just a little bit more so that your fellow West Virginians will not have to suffer."

Alert for their cue, four pretty teenage girls appeared at the back of the hall and marched down the middle and side aisles carrying brand-new milk buckets, courtesy of GRINNELL'S HARDWARE STORE. When they reached the front of the hall, each turned and commenced passing her bucket down one row of seats and collecting the bucket that reached her coming down the next row. In this manner, the girls slowly worked their way to the back of the hall, men and women dropping coins and sometimes a dollar bill into the buckets, so that by the time the last row was reached each bucket was more than half full.

"Are you ready now to hear some of the best fiddling this side of Jordan?" the mayor shouted as the girls swinging their buckets filed out into the lobby where Maury Taylor, the club's treasurer, awaited them with a stack of cloth sacks, the words KANAWHA VALLEY BANK stenciled on each one.

Inside the hall there were more hoots and hollers. The mayor was having a spanking good time.

"Then let me call onto the stage our first contestant. The order was determined by drawing lots, and each contestant will play a breakdown followed by a waltz."

A man in his fifties with a drooping mustache sauntered out unto the stage. He held a blond violin and pinned to the back of his red gingham shirt was a square of paper with the number 1 printed on it. He was accompanied by a guitar player who carried himself with a limp.

The crowd grew silent as the fiddler launched into a spirited rendition of *Billy in the Low Ground*. He followed this up with *The Fifty-Years-Ago Waltz*, known also as *The Anniversary Waltz*. The next to play in the contest was a short, balding fiddler whose excited blue eyes shone like those of a child on Christmas morning. He already had ribbons streaming from the scroll of his fiddle, having won or placed in previous contests in other towns. He offered up his music to the judges and the audience unaccompanied: *Fisher's Hornpipe* followed by *Lorena*, which, although not a waltz, elicited spirited applause.

Thus it continued throughout the evening. Many of the contestants were dressed to the nines, as befitted the occasion, with starched collars and freshly polished shoes. A few, however, wore bib overalls, as if they had just walked from the milking barn to the stage. One fiddler was blind, and he held his fiddle and bow in one hand so he could rest his other on his wife's shoulder as she led him to the center of the stage. He then played the fiddle while she played backup on the banjo.

It was nearly midnight before the last breakdown and waltz were played, and then the party continued into the early hours of the morning in hotel rooms throughout the city.

Now it happened that one of the fiddlers, contestant number 12, was a farmer named Shelby Armstrong. He lived near Oak Hill, West Virginia, and operated a ninety-acre dairy farm that he had inherited from his father. But it was his Uncle Brice, his mother's brother, who taught him how to play the violin. The uncle lived for some years down in the Ozarks, so Shelby knew some lively Missouri tunes as well as most of the West Virginia standards. All the same, Shelby had never played in a contest before. And he wouldn't have played in the Charleston contest if it hadn't been for his neighbors who urged him to.

"You're as good and a darn sight better than most of them city fiddlers," boasted Dale Appleton, who ran the feed store where Shelby traded. "Why, the tunes you played at Miss Guthrie's wedding were some of the prettiest I've ever heard. Isn't that right, Marlen?"

Marlen James, another dairyman, nodded his head in agreement. "Go up there and make us proud of you, Shelby. I'll send my boy Walter over to help with the milking while you're away."

Shelby thought it over and had to admit that December was as good a month as any to go off on a frolic. He was caught up with his farm work, except for feeding and milking the cows, which had no end.

"What the heck," he told himself. "Maybe I can show them boys up in Charleston a thing or two."

So Shelby had his wife drive him to the station where he could catch the train that would carry him to Charleston.

"You take care of yourself, dear," his wife said as she handed him a poke containing of couple of sandwiches and three apples. "Don't run off with some floozy."

Shelby didn't care much for trains, the clatter of the cars and the way coal smoke would blow back in through the windows; some fool was always opening a window, even in the winter. Sitting across from him was a drummer who peddled sewing notions and rubber galoshes.

"I always wanted to learn to play the violin," the man said eyeing the fiddle case on the seat next to Shelby. "Do you play professionally?"

"I just play here and there," Shelby said. "Mostly for fun."

"Take your fiddle everywhere you go?"

He sure is a busybody, Shelby thought. He was having trouble placing the drummer's accent but suspected the man was a Yankee.

"I'm on my way to play in a fiddle contest."

"A fellow drummer told me about that contest. When is it?"

"Tomorrow night at the Odd Fellows Hall."

"The Odd Fellows Hall? You don't say. Why, I might just go."

"There's nothing to stop you unless they've sold out the tickets."

"That won't be a problem," the man bragged, flashing a smile, a pair of gold crowns glittering from back in his mouth. "I'm well liked in Charleston. A salesman's got to be, if he hopes to get on. What line of work are you in, if you don't mind me asking?"

"I'm a dairyman."

"A dairyman? You don't say. Why, my pappy was a dairyman. And his biggest complaint was how the rain and manure kept ruining his shoes. Why, I just happen to represent a line of high-quality galoshes. They're made from the sap of rubber trees that grow along the Amazon River in South America . . ."

The agitation of the contest was now over and Shelby found himself lying in bed in the hotel, staring up at the ceiling, unable to sleep. He had gone up against some tip-top fiddlers and come away empty-handed. Maybe he should have played that Missouri tune, the one called *Jimmy in the Swamp*. He had added a dandy third part to the tune several months earlier and changed the name to *Devil in the Swamp*

With His Corncob Pipe. The title alone would have caught the judges' attention. Instead, he played it safe: *Blackberry Blossom* for his breakdown and *The Gold and Silver Waltz* for his slow tune.

"Stop fussing about what's over and done with," he scolded himself. "You can't do a blessed thing about it now."

But late night worries are hard to tame, and his thoughts turned to the sorry state of his wallet. He added up the price of the train ticket, lodging for two nights, and the cost of his meals, plus the entry fee for the contest, which, at two dollars, was nothing to sneeze at.

The room was warm and stuffy, so he got up and opened the window. But instead of frigid air, a pleasant, warm breeze wafted in and brushed his skin. The moon, almost full, rose above the rooftops of the city and shone like the headlamp of a locomotive. That gave him an idea. He could save the cost of a return train ticket by making the journey home to Oak Hill on foot. He had made the footslog twice in the past, although both times had been during the summer. All the same, given how unseasonably warm it was, he calculated he could make the trip in two days, arriving home late on the evening of the second day. He could find some farmer willing to put him up for a night, and, if not, he had a thick coat and could sleep out of doors. "Yep, that's what I'm going to do," he muttered to himself as he at last drifted off to sleep.

Shelby Armstrong set off at the crack of dawn and by mid-day he was south of Charleston, where the road began to wind its way up into the mountains. It had grown so warm he was beginning to sweat, which made him laugh because Christmas was only a couple of weeks away.

A bootblack in the city had sold him a strip of leather, which he attached to his fiddle case so he could sling it over his shoulder. He had also cut himself a staff from a hickory sapling to ward off any dogs or snakes he might encounter.

The road climbed steadily into a forest leaving the farms and villages of the Kanawha Valley behind. For two hours he made good progress, passing only one homestead that was protected by a barking yellow mongrel, and that, minding the hickory staff, stopped at the gate to the yard. The afternoon was well advanced and Shelby considered approaching the owner and asking if he could camp out in his barn. But he didn't like the look of the snarling, ill-mannered canine and knew that owners often take after their dogs. Besides, he reasoned, if he kept going he would likely come upon another farm before nightfall and be that much closer to home.

As he trudged along he began to hum a fiddle tune to himself. It was called *Rye Straw* and had four parts, the second and fourth parts being nearly the same. Then he realized *Rye Straw* was the tune the winner of the fiddle contest had played. The man played all the notes and then some, but Shelby thought his bowing of the third part was on the raggedy side. But it didn't matter what he thought. The crowd and judges loved the man's playing and sent him home to Youngstown, Ohio, with fifty dollars in his pocket and a blue silk ribbon to hang from the scroll of his violin.

Shelby quit humming *Rye Straw* and switched over to *Cold Frosty Morning*. Now, maybe it was nothing more than coincidence, but as he hummed the tune the wind kicked up and the temperature began to drop. It dropped so fast, in fact, that it caught Shelby by surprise. The first thing he noticed was that he had stopped sweating. More than that, he had begun to shiver. He stopped walking long enough to button up his coat. All about him were dark, silent trees, the road under his feet the only sign of human endeavor.

"I don't care for this weather," he addressed the mute trees, "maybe I should turn back." But that meant walking two hours in the wrong direction and then maybe the farmer with the barking dog would take him in, or maybe he wouldn't. No, he would press on. He should reach the pass soon, where he remembered there was a hotel. He couldn't recall the name, but he had spent the night there once and recalled it as tolerable.

He began walking again, quickening his step, but had not gone far when the wind began to stiffen. One powerful gust blew his hat off, and he had to chase after it and snatch it off the ground. He jammed the hat back on his head and soldiered on, but seeds of worry were germinating inside his mind. What if he got caught out in a winter storm? He knew the weather was fickle in December. Had he been a fool to try and cross the high mountains without the guarantee of shelter?

He slipped his free hand into the pocket of his coat hoping to find some matches. All he fished out was a ball of lint and two Indian head pennies. Why hadn't he thought to bring matches?

"Because," he told himself, "you allowed brooding over the loss of the fiddle contest to distract you. Well, there is nothing you can do about it now."

Shelby pulled up his coat collar; the wind was stronger and beginning to spit small flakes of icy snow into his eyes.

"The hotel can't be much farther," he muttered, keeping his head down so as not to lose his hat again.

The road was now white with snow, the falling, swirling

flakes getting larger and heavier the higher he climbed. Again he quickened his pace, ignoring the protests of his thigh and calf muscles. He began to sing *The Devil and the Farmer's Wife*. It was an old ditty that his mother used to sing, and it told how the devil one day carried a farmer's wife down to hell only to find that she intended to wreck the place, killing a peck of little demons in the bargain, so he had to lug her back home again. Shelby liked the last two verses the best:

> *"I've been a devil all of my life,*
> *But I've never been in hell till I met your wife."*
> *Sing fi, diddle aye, diddle aye, dee,*
> *diddle aye diddle aye, dae.*

> *"And that proves that women are better than men,*
> *They can go down to hell and come back again.*
> *Sing fi, diddle aye, diddle aye, dee,*
> *diddle aye diddle aye, dae."*

The snap of branch off to his right made him stop and turn. Was it the storm or a bear? Maybe a panther. He peered into the forest looking for the glint of malevolent eyes, but all was dark, cold emptiness. He trudged on. Singing *The Devil and the Farmer's Wife* usually worked to cheer him up; it was the only time when he was a kid he could say the word "hell" and not feel the sting of the switch. But this time singing the song just seemed like work and he abandoned the effort.

His right foot slipped on the snow, but the hickory staff kept him from falling. Exhaustion was turning his legs to wood, his feet into numb mallets beating the snowy ground with every step. He was tempted to leave the road and seek shelter in among the trees. He was so tired, but he knew that to fall asleep was to never again awaken.

Step after step, each an effort of will. He stopped and scooped up a handful of snow and wet his lips. He threw aside his walking stick and thrust his smarting hands into his pockets. Even the violin that hung about his neck was a burden. He kept pulling on the strap to shift the weight. It was the violin's fault. What a conceited fool he was to believe he could win the contest. And to waste all that money on a train ticket and a room and the entry fee. Come the spring, with a little luck, he would sell enough calves to recoup the loss.

He continued walking. His fatigue was such that he could sense the slightest change in the grade of the road, and after another mile he felt it begin to level out. That meant he was nearing the pass. Up ahead was a clearing. And yes, there, against the now dark sky he could just make out the silhouette of a large building. The sight gave his spirits a tremendous lift and the weariness fell from his limbs. He began to jog, but as he drew nigh unto the hotel he became puzzled, because he saw no lights burning. Maybe the shutters were closed to keep out the storm. The wind had begun to twist and howl and conjure up swirling ghost-like shapes from the snow that lay on the ground.

At last Shelby reached the building and climbed the steps onto the porch. He tried the door, but it was locked. He banged on the door with his fist. The insistent cold pushed deep into his bones and made him sleepy. He put his hand on the doorknob again and tried to turn it, the cold metal grabbing the skin of his palm and not letting go. Then he attempted to force the door open, but the lock held firm. He slid down into a sitting position with his back to the door, and pulled his coat around him as tightly as he could. The air smelled of snow and pine resin, fingers of wind reached in under the eaves to both mock and caress him. His head fell forward on his chest as sleep, at last, overtook him.

Monday morning, after the storm played itself out, Willis Plumbly trotted up over the pass with his saddlebags full of mail for the settlement of Soap Creek three miles further south. He reined in his horse when he noticed a dark shape on the porch of the Mountain Laurel. He studied the shape, but cautiously, in case it was a rabid animal of some kind. When it didn't move, he spurred his horse forward. And there on the porch, he found a man huddled up in a heap and covered with a thin layer of snow blown in on top of him during the storm. Next to the man was a violin case; it too dusted with fresh snow. Willis dismounted and attempted to rouse the man.

"Wake up, fellow," Willis said as he shook the man's shoulder. "Is something wrong? Are you sick?"

When this elicited no response, Willis removed his glove and touched the man's face. It was stiff and cold as a block of ice. He unbuttoned the stranger's coat and put his ear on the man's chest and listened for a heartbeat. There was none.

Willis said a short prayer for the benefit of the unfortunate man's soul. He then remounted his horse and set off to summon help.

As you can imagine, the news of the fiddler's death caused quite a stir in that part of the country with everyone keen to discover the stranger's identity. The sheriff telegraphed the man's description to towns throughout the region, and two days later Shelby Armstrong's wife and his brother Matt arrived with a horse and buckboard wagon to claim the body. It was a sad affair, but life, like a mountain stream, flows on.

Come the following March, Grumgenhoff returned to the Mountain Laurel and set about getting the hotel ready and open for business. What he discovered, however, and much to his annoyance, was that people only cared to talk about one thing: the fiddler's untimely death.

"It's an awful shame the way that man died trying to get into your hotel," a neighbor would say to Grumgenhoff.

"It is not my fault," an angry Grumgenhoff would reply, "the fool had no more sense than a turnip, trying to cross the mountains that time of year."

"No one blames you," the neighbor would hasten to placate the irate innkeeper, while relishing the rise he had gotten out of the old sourpuss.

Grumgenhoff, meanwhile, filled his larder and aired the rooms, and the first night the hotel was open he counted a dozen lodgers. He fed everyone and waited until they finished their smokes and went to bed before banking the coals in the large fireplace of the common room, locking up, and going to bed himself. He had no trouble falling asleep, but he was awakened sometime later by a queer sound. He lit the candle he kept next to the bed and looked at his watch. It was just on midnight and he could hear the standing clock downstairs in the hallway chiming the hour. The other sound, the one that woke him, was someone playing the fiddle. This made him angry because he enforced strict rules when it came to music-making after ten o'clock at night. Once he turned a luckless drummer out into the night with a weighty clout to the man's ear because he was drunk and wouldn't stop playing his French harp. There was no arguing with Otto Grumgenhoff when his blood was up.

Throwing his stout legs over the side of the bed, he stood and pulled on his robe. He tugged the belt tight about his generous torso, picked up the candle, and started down the upstairs hallway meaning to have it out with the inconsiderate and, he suspected, inebriated fiddler who would annoy the other guests at such an hour.

Grumgenhoff, however, discerned that the music wasn't issuing from any of the upstairs guest rooms as he expected, so he went to the top of the stairs and listened. No question about it. The music was coming from downstairs—and not just downstairs, but from inside his office across the hallway from the foot of the stairs. This discovery fueled his wrath, but puzzled him, too, because he always kept the door to his office locked and he couldn't understand how someone could have gotten inside.

He clomped down the stairs, the candle held out in front of him so he wouldn't trip, while the fiddle music played on, a plaintive and lonesome sound, not at all the kind of tune you would expect from a man well into his cups.

Reaching the bottom of the stairs, Grumgenhoff crossed the hall and tried to open the door to his office, but it was locked, as it should be. He reached into the pocket of his robe and removed a ring of keys. His hand trembled with rage as he thumbed through the keys to find the right one. He pictured in his mind the hickory ax handle he kept leaning against the wall just inside the office, next to the door. If there was to be a physical confrontation, he was ready for it. Taking a deep breath, he fit the key into the lock, turned it, and pushed open the door.

The music stopped—abruptly—the faint echo of the melody fading away to nothingness. Grumgenhoff held the candle aloft so that he might peer into the corners where the shadows cowered. But he saw no one. The room was empty. He stepped forward and moved the candle from side to side surveying the condition of the office. Everything appeared normal, until he came around behind his desk, where he discovered that someone had rifled through the drawers and littered the floor with their contents.

Grumgenhoff struggled to make sense of what he saw. Had he interrupted a burglary? If so, then where was the burglar? He went to the windows and checked them. They, like the door, were locked. And why would a burglar call attention to himself by playing music? It made no sense at all.

For the next half hour, Grumgenhoff conducted a thorough inventory of the papers and items in his desk, and, as far as he could tell, nothing was missing. Eventually he went back to bed, but he slept fitfully, his contentment undermined by troubled dreams that, like the mysterious fiddler in his office, flitted away just out of reach through the passageways of his unconscious mind.

The next night, the same thing happened again. At the stroke of twelve, Grumgenhoff was awakened by the sound of music. Again he got up and followed the sound until it led him to his office, where, with a sinking heart, he unlocked the door and pushed it open only to find the room empty. This time, however, it wasn't his desk that had been violated. The top drawer of the filing cabinet against the wall was pulled out and papers scattered all over the floor. But after further inspection, Grumgenhoff determined that nothing had been taken.

Thus it continued each and every night. The fiddle music would begin at midnight, always mournful and yet full of yearning, and it would draw Grumgenhoff downstairs to his office where he would discover that some other part of the office had been ransacked and yet nothing was ever missing.

And it wasn't just the innkeeper who heard the soul-chilling music. The guests heard it too, and word spread faster than rabbits in a pea patch that the hotel was haunted by the ghost of the fiddler who froze to death on the porch of the hotel. That is what people believed and who could blame them? But it was an explanation Grumgenhoff refused to accept. He convinced himself that it just was a mean-spirited prank, an elaborate practical joke, and he would get to the bottom of it, and then watch out! The culprits would pay and pay dearly.

Still, the ghost story proved a disaster for his business. Within a week, people stopped coming to his hotel. Nobody dared spend the night in the company of some restless spirit. What if the fiddler got bored with haunting the innkeeper's office and decided to visit one of the guest rooms? This possibility was too much for people, so they stayed away.

For several nights, Grumgenhoff refused to get up when he heard the music. He just lay in bed with his pillow wrapped tight around his head in a vain attempt to block it out. And on those nights when he didn't get up and go downstairs, the music continued unabated all night long and only stopped with the coming of dawn, always the same heartbreaking melody, played over and over again. It threatened to drive the poor German crazy.

Then one day Willis Plumbly stopped at the Mountain Laurel to deliver a letter from Grumgenhoff's sister, and the sight of the hotel owner was enough to stop his breath. Grumgenhoff had lost so much weight and color that Willis scarcely recognized him. His hollowed-out eyes had a crazed cast to them that caused the mail carrier genuine concern.

"There's a woman hereabouts who might be able to help you get shut of that ghost of yours," he told Grumgenhoff.

"There is no ghost," Grumgenhoff replied, his voice flat and distant.

"Her name is Rennie Sharewood. I'm sure you've heard of her."

Grumgenhoff had often heard people talk about the Sharewood woman, but he had never met her. When adults spoke her name, they did so with respect. Not so the children. They were convinced Rennie Sharewood was a witch, because she was old and she lived off in the mountains by herself and talked and acted strangely. "She knows things," they whispered to each other, "secret things."

And in some ways this was true, because Rennie knew more about the wild plants that grew in that part of the country than anyone else. If you had a toothache, she would make you a paste to rub on the gum near the offending tooth, and the pain went away, at least long enough so you could get to a dentist or work up the courage to yank the tooth yourself. For lice, she made a powder by grinding the bark of a certain tree and it did the trick every time. The lice packed their bags and hunted up some other poor scalp on which to dine.

But most of the time it was an anxious husband or midwife who sent for Rennie to help with a birth. She would come and brew up an odd-smelling concoction made from herbs and roots that helped relieve the pain and make the birthing go easier. This set the doctors against her and some preachers, too, because the Bible taught that Eve tempted Adam to eat of the forbidden fruit and part of her punishment was that all women must suffer the pain of childbirth. Anyone, therefore, who interfered with God's judgment in this regard must be wicked and of the Devil. One mountain preacher, the Reverend Albion T. Snodgrass, a dyspeptic man with a hooked nose and eyebrows like woolly worms, preached against the old woman regularly from his pulpit and that is probably where the children picked up the idea that she was a witch. Most people, however, regarded Snodgrass as cracked and were sincerely glad to have a wise woman like Rennie Sharewood living in the vicinity.

For some time, Grumgenhoff refused to go to the old woman for help, but in the end it got so bad he had no choice. It was either that or burn down the hotel.

So one Saturday morning, he screwed up his nerve and set out for Rennie's place. As he marched up through the small meadow that sloped down from her hewn-log cabin, he spied her sitting on her porch, rocking back and forth in a chair, facing his direction as if she had been expecting him all along. This impression gave Grumgenhoff the jumps.

"Miss Sharewood," he said as he reached her, "I am Otto Grumgenhoff. I own—"

"I know who you are," she cut him off, her dark eyes fixed on his, "and I've a pretty good notion why you're here."

She motioned to an empty chair next to her and he sat down. She struck a match on the arm of her chair and held it up to the bowl of a corncob pipe. She sucked on the pipe until her mouth filled with smoke and then blew it out in a narrow stream. Grumgenhoff took this as a signal to tell his story. She didn't interrupt him, just puffed on her pipe and smiled now and again, revealing her nut-brown, tobacco-stained teeth. He noticed her skin, too, which had acquired the hue and texture of old saddle leather from spending so much time out-of-doors collecting the ingredients for her special potions.

He finished his tale. He wasn't one to story much, as I've said, but when it came to the invisible fiddler he gave Rennie the information right down to the details. The old woman stopped rocking and set her pipe down. She closed her eyes for a long minute, allowing the sounds of the natural world to press in upon them. Birds sang to each other and bees buzzed about their business as a light breeze swept through the leaves of the trees next to the cabin, like a hand brushing a dog's coat.

Finally she opened her eyes and spoke.

"You have yerself a ghost, Mr. Grumgenhoff, no question about that."

He started to disagree, but a sharp look from her made him shut his mouth, his words gathered up captive behind his teeth like Odysseus and his men inside the Cyclops' cave.

"And ghosts can be tricky," she continued. "From what you tell me, it's a-lookin' for somethin' in your office, and to get shut of it we've got to puzzle out what it's a-lookin' for."

He noted how she referred to the ghost as an "it," not a "him" or "her." He guessed she no longer regarded ghosts as people. Instead, they were a force, like a flowing creek or lightning during a storm. One dealt with them, when one had to, as one would with any natural phenomenon. This practical approach did much to dispel the panic that had threatened for months to overwhelm Grumgenhoff's mind.

"So tell me, what do you keep in that room of yours that it wants?"

Grumgenhoff was at a loss and all he could do was shrug. "Just ordinary things: bills, lists of supplies, correspondence, some recipes," he said.

"Then it must be something hidden away, or it would have found it by now."

His thoughts ambled until he remembered something.

"I keep a metal strongbox hidden under a loose floor board in that room," he said and Rennie's eyes shone with excitement and she leaned toward him, her right hand cradling her chin.

"What's inside the box?" she demanded.

"Legal papers . . . the deed to the property . . . and money. Is it wanting my money?" he asked.

Disdain washed over the old woman's sharp features and she shook her head.

"What use has it got for your money?" she said. "There's no need for money in the world where it's a-goin'. Is there nothing else in that box of yours?"

His mind now galloped like a startled pony. The box. The papers. The money. The loose floorboard. The money. There, on top of the money. Made of brass. Kept in the box until needed in the fall.

"The key to the hotel," he blurted out. "I keep the key for the front door in the box. Is that what it wants?"

The old woman smacked her knee and threw her head back with a yelp of triumph that made the innkeeper start.

"By jingo, that's it! That's what it's been a-lookin' for, sure as the world, the key to open the door so it won't die out there in the cold all alone. Desperate it must have been in them last moments, still wanting to live and all."

She locked eyes with the anxious innkeeper. "And I've a pretty good notion that you've got to give the key to the spirit yourself, in person. That's what it wants, it surely does. You can bet good money on it."

"I am not betting money on anything!" Grumgenhoff exclaimed, jumping up and knocking his chair backwards with clatter. He was blazing with indignation mixed with terror. He was not going to give any *key* to any *ghost*. Besides, there was no ghost. He saw it now. She was part of the prank, along with Plumbly and the rest. They all hated him because he wouldn't laugh at their stupid jokes or share in their poisonous gossip. They were a narrow-minded, backward people consumed by superstition and envy. What they really aimed to do was drive him away so they could have the Mountain Laurel all for themselves. His heart burned with hatred for the mail carrier who had sent him on this wasted, foolhardy journey.

He trod down the grass and wildflowers as he started for home through the meadow. He refused to look back, even though he could feel the old woman watching him as she rocked back and forth on her porch, grinning like a possum with those nut-brown teeth of hers. She was surely mocking him.

When he got back to the hotel all he could do was go from one empty room to the next, slamming doors behind him and looking for things to kick. Later, he couldn't make his supper without breaking two dishes. Never had he been this upset and more than once he caught himself grinding his teeth. And through all this upheaval he kept hearing the old woman's voice in his head, "And I've a notion that you've got to give the key to it yourself, in person. That's what it wants, it surely does."

After supper he tried to read but couldn't keep his eyes focused on the letters, they kept hopping about like unruly children. He finally gave up and flung the book across the room. He went upstairs to bed. But sleep evaded him. He tossed and turned until the clock downstairs chimed eleven times. One hour until midnight. Then came the single chime for the half-hour—11:30—and suddenly the mask of anger fell from his heart and he accepted with both dread and humility what had to be done. The old woman was right. He must confront his tormentor. One more night of the ghostly fiddle music and he would as likely cut his throat as put a bullet through his head.

So, getting up out of bed, he relit the candle, put on his robe, and went out the door of his bedroom. He walked past the vacant guest rooms until he came to the top of the stairs and looked down into the darkness. The fiddler would come soon. With a sigh, Grumgenhoff descended the stairs slowly with the measured, reluctant tread of a prisoner going to the gallows. Once inside his office, he set his candle on the desk and pulled open the bottom drawer. Inside was an old military bayonet that he had brought with him from Germany when he deserted the army. He removed the bayonet from the drawer and used it to pry up the loose floorboard. He pulled out the metal strongbox and opened it. There, weighing down a stack of greenbacks, was the large brass key. He took the key and placed it on top of the desk next to the candle. He moved around to the other side of the desk and sat down so that he faced the closed door of his office. He commenced to waiting. All was silence except for the faint ticking of the standing clock in the hallway.

Midnight arrived. The clock began to chime. One, two, three, four—the door to the office swung noiselessly open and the room grew cold with the bleak, damp chill of a disused cellar or tomb. Grumgenhoff watched transfixed as the flame of the candle wavered, as if responding to a breeze no mortal flesh could feel. All the while the clock continued its appointed task—ten, eleven, twelve.

He sensed something, not with his eyes, but some presence now stood motionless on the far side of the desk, waiting.

He tried to swallow but his tongue was mortared in place, his mouth dry as dust. He could not speak even if he wanted to. Then with a great effort of will, he reached out for the key that lay on top of the desk. Invisible, insistent eyes bore into his very soul as he commanded his fingers to open and take hold of the key. In a supreme act of determination, he half rose from the chair and extended his arm with the key toward the ghost, his legs trembling and near to buckling from the weight of horror that bore down on him.

When, suddenly, without warning—

WHOOSH!

His hand burst into flames, as hot and bright as the sun. Searing pain rocked his senses. His mind reeled. Half-blinded, he shrieked and yanked his hand back, violently, falling backwards with an anguished moan into his chair. The pain and the blinding light were the last things he remembered.

The next morning, as the warm golden sunlight of a summer morning poured in through the windows of his office and birds chirped gaily outside, Grumgenhoff regained consciousness. His mind was a fog of distraught dreams and agitated emotions. Then his mind regained its focus and the memories flooded in: the clock striking midnight, the door of his office swinging open by itself, the cold, damp air, and the invisible presence on the far side of the desk, waiting. Then came the memory of his hand exploding into flames and the intense pain. He looked down at his hand in his lap. It was charred black. He tried to move his fingers and the pain made him wince. He looked for the key on the desk, but it wasn't there. Made of brass, it could not have caught fire. He was drunk on confusion. He held his damaged hand up against his chest, gingerly, and managed to get down on his knees so he could search the floor for the key. He never found it. The key was gone.

And so was the ghost of the fiddler. Never again would its lamenting music haunt the owner and guests of the Mountain Laurel.

It took time for Grumgenhoff's hand to heal. Thankfully, no infection set in, and he regained the use of it. Word soon spread that ghost had departed, and the hotel was once more filled with contented guests.

As to the question of whether people can change, Otto Grumgenhoff *was* that changed man. Where before he had been dour and quick to suspect others of low motives or incompetence, he now fostered a sunnier disposition. Not only was he friendlier, he was chattier. This, of course, was welcomed by one and all, and guests now felt comfortable staying up late telling stories and swapping jokes, and yes, even singing songs and playing music, because from the innkeeper there came no word of admonition, not even a raised eyebrow. Quite the opposite, in fact. Grumgenhoff now joined in the merrymaking.

The innkeeper also no longer left during the winter months but kept the hotel open year-round, even though he had few guests after the snows came. When he did go away for a day or two, he made sure never to lock the front door. Someone might come by and rob him, but that was a risk he was willing to take. He just wanted to make sure that if someone needed to get into the hotel for any reason he would never again find the door locked against him. That is the lesson Grumgenhoff learned from the phantom fiddler, one he never forgot.

In fact, he took pleasure in telling the story about the ghost and the unearthly fiddle music. The telling usually took place late at night just before the guests went up to bed. He would extinguish the oil lamps and light a single candle and someone would say, "Tell us, Otto, about the man who froze to death on the porch of this hotel."

And Grumgenhoff would tell the tale in a quiet, steady voice calculated to draw his listeners in very close, so that when he finished and held out his right hand they could see across his palm, illuminated by the light of the candle, a thick white scar. And the shape of that scar was the very likeness of a large brass key.

SAILOR'S
HORNPIPE

Rain blew through the window as the carriage turned onto
Front Street, and Sarah Gallagher loosened the cord securing
the rubberized canvas shade and let it drop. The storm had
come up suddenly from the south, the tropical Florida sky
blue and laughing one moment, gray and weeping the next.
Eight days earlier she had been sitting in a New England
college classroom reading Shakespeare's *Twelfth Night*, her
heart carefree in the way only a youthful heart can be. Then
the telegram arrived informing her that her grandfather had
died. Her friend Millie accompanied her to the train station
and found a porter to handle her bags.

"Travel safely," Millie yelled over a blast of steam issuing
from beneath the locomotive, "we will miss you."

Then it was a day, a night, and another day on the
train, heading south. Sarah slept poorly, the Pullman
compartment hot and stuffy, the pull-down bed narrow and
hard. Memories flowed through her like a river, at times
serene and wide, but then churning and flecked with sorrow.

She recalled walking along the beach with her grandfather when she was a young child, stopping now and again to pick up periwinkle shells and pieces of bleached driftwood, the hem of retreating waves scooping sand from around her small feet.

When she was older, they would go deep-sea fishing together, just the two of them. Her job was to pour water from a long-handled cup onto the giant reel whenever a blue marlin took the bait. Fish that big and strong pulled away so fast the friction could snap the line if it wasn't kept cool. To tire the fish, her grandfather would wrench the stout rod backward until its tip pointed toward the sky, then allow it to drop again so he could reel in more line. He repeated this motion over and over as the day wore on until finally the great silver body glided in surrender just beneath the surface of the water next to the boat.

She also enjoyed their trips into the Everglades, where she once watched a one-eyed man wrestle an alligator; the spectacle of the thrashing monster snapping its long, toothy mouth both thrilled and frightened her.

"You must be careful around alligators, Sarah, but don't be afraid of them," he told her. "They are part of God's creation, same as you and me."

But her favorite moments were at night, when she squeezed in next to him in the big leather chair in the library. There, wreathed in the sweet aroma of his pipe tobacco, she listened and dreamed as he spun yarns about mermaids and shipwrecks and faraway lands.

This was the man no one in the family knew but her. With the rest, he was taciturn, letting his sister, when she came to visit, run the show. Sarah never knew her grandmother; she died long before Sarah was born. It was whispered she was

a Seminole princess. Others said her grandfather met his
future wife while climbing the mountains of Peru and that
her father was an Inca priest.

Sarah put little stock in these rumors. How could she?
There were so many of them. One popular bit of gossip
claimed her grandfather had once been a slave trader. Other
rumors, in no particular order of importance, claimed
he had been a counterfeiter, a briber of public officials, a
professional gambler, and an opium dealer. Papa *was* rich,
there was no denying that, but he wasn't puffed up like the
other rich people she knew, including her parents. She had
read in a newspaper once that Thomas Gallagher was the
wealthiest man in Florida and that no ambitious politician
could hope to get elected governor or United States senator
without first securing his support. His commercial interests,
the newspaper reported, included real estate, shipping,
sugar plantations, sponging, orange groves, and oil wells.
But the big question always remained: where did he first get
his money? Speculation on this topic was boundless but her
grandfather refused to discuss it with anyone, even with his
own family.

"Let them yammer," he laughed once when she asked if
the rumors bothered him. "People need something to chew
on. Otherwise, they get antsy and cause real mischief. Talk
cannot hurt you if you don't let it."

And that is all he would say on the subject, which was fine
with her. She loved him and he loved her. Her parents were
caught up in the intrigues and frivolities of high society,
and had scant time for their only child, who they judged
to be a clever girl but far too shy. Except for Lucille, her
black nanny, Sarah spent much of her childhood alone. Her
favorite season was winter, when her parents sent her south

to stay with her grandfather. Despite the years that separated them, Papa was her best friend and trusted confidante, right up until the day she went off to college. Then she made new friends, like Millie, and Papa's health began to fail. The days slipped by unnoticed, and it became harder to find time to visit, what with the demands of her schoolwork and her summer job as a camp counselor and swimming instructor. Then news came that he was gone. Bitter salt tears burned her cheeks as she stared out the window of the passenger car, the fields and woods slipping by, obscured now and again by gray shrouds of smoke from the hardworking locomotive.

The warm Key West rain ceased as the carriage pulled up in front of the law offices of Bryson, Tenhullzen and Drake.

"Sorry for the mud, miss," the driver apologized as he helped her down unto the sidewalk.

"Not the best time of year to visit south Florida. It's either too hot and humid, or it's raining to beat the band."

"Thank you," she said as she handed him the fare. The man slipped the money into his vest pocket, tipped his hat, and climbed back up onto the carriage.

Sarah turned the polished brass doorknob and entered the law office. The day before, she had stood and watched as they lowered her grandfather into the ground and the sight of that had very nearly broken her heart. Now the family was gathering for the reading of the will and the dispersion of his estate—his businesses, bank accounts, and personal belongings—before hurrying back to the embrace of the world.

For Sarah, that world now felt empty and cold. She had heard that the souls of the deceased lingered before quitting this earthly plane, and, as she approached a young man working at his desk, she wondered if her grandfather's spirit might still be present. She sniffed and thought she caught the scent of Papa's brand of pipe tobacco. This eased her heart; she felt that grandfather was near.

"I'm here to see Mr. Bryson," she said to the young man. He was typing a letter on a large black machine that clattered like a troop of mattock-wielding leprechauns digging coal.

Caught unawares, he jumped at the sound of her voice, his fingers frozen above the round porcelain keys.

"I'm sorry," he stammered, trying collecting his wits, "I didn't hear you come in."

He looked at her intently and she noticed flecks of gray in his hazel eyes. She had never seen eyes quite like his.

"My name is—"

"Yes, I know. You are Miss Sarah Gallagher. They are waiting for you."

He stood up and buttoned his frock coat and then smoothed the front with his hands.

"I am Mr. Hall, Anthony Hall, Mr. Bryson's assistant. Your grandfather was an exceptional man. Allow me to offer my condolences."

"Thank you," she said.

"I didn't know your grandfather all that well, but he was a fine gentleman and generous to those less fortunate."

"Yes," she replied, "he was a kind man."

He stared at her as if distracted by something and the silence between them grew.

"Has anyone else arrived?" Sarah asked, breaking the spell.

"Oh yes. They are in the conference room with Mr. Bryson. If you'd care to follow me."

He led her down a thickly carpeted hallway to a door. He knocked softly and opened the door.

Inside, seated at a mahogany table, were her parents. Recently divorced, they were an unhappy pair: her father smoking an expensive cigar, impatient as always, her mother looking old and worn despite the ministration of expensive cosmetics. Seated next to her father was her Great Aunt Gertrude, a buxom, jovial woman of eighty-three who favored large hats made even larger by a profusion of bird feathers and silk flowers and who, because of ill-fitting dentures, whistled when she spoke.

"There you are, my dear," Aunt Gertrude called out. "What a sad day this is for all of us. Come, sit by me." She patted the cushion of the empty chair next to her, the jeweled rings on her fingers clinking together as she did so.

Sarah went over and kissed her aunt on the cheek before sitting down. Her parents made a brief nod in her direction but didn't speak, their attention trained on the lawyer.

Mr. Bryson, her grandfather's attorney, was a tall, mildly cadaverous man in a starched collar, blue cravat with diamond stickpin, and pince-nez. To his right, facing her parents and aunt, were three people: Miss Hollins, her grandfather's housekeeper of many years, Mr. Garabino, the gardener and sometimes chauffeur, and a middle-aged man with heavy eyebrows and a ruddy, uneven complexion who she had seen at the funeral but to whom she had not been introduced.

"I trust you are well, Miss Gallagher," Mr. Bryson said. "No doubt these last days have been trying."

"I hope I have not kept you waiting," Sarah replied.

"Not at all. Your aunt and I have been catching up on old times. I met your grandfather sixty years ago when I first came to Key West. I was a young man trying to make my way in the law and your grandfather, who had a considerable fortune even then, sought my advice on how best to structure his investments. To this day, I don't know why he chose me to oversee his interests, but we got along well and, as you know, his businesses flourished.

"My brother knew how to make a dollar; there's no shame in that," Aunt Gertrude added.

Sarah's father shot a sharp, irritated glance at his aunt but kept the cigar clamped between his teeth and said nothing.

"I believe you know Mrs. Hollins and Mr. Garabino," Mr. Bryson said. "This is Mr. Smythe. He is a director of the Sailors' Retirement Home here in Key West."

"You grandfather was a great man, Miss Gallagher," Smythe said. "He will be sorely missed."

The man's gruff but straightforward manner appealed to Sarah and she smiled.

"Did you know my grandfather well?" she asked.

"As well as any man could, I venture to say. But your grandfather did have his secrets."

These last words hung in the air until Mr. Bryson intervened.

"Yes, well, we are not here to discuss secrets but to read Mr. Gallagher's last will and testament. If no one objects, I will begin."

He picked up an envelope, slipped a letter opener under the flap, and sliced it open. He then withdrew a single sheet of paper.

Adjusting his pince-nez, he began to read:

"I, Thomas Gladdius Gallagher, being of sound mind and body, do upon my death hereby bequeath the following: To my son Bernard, I leave the sum of ten thousand dollars. I would give him a great deal more but all he has ever cared for in this world is money, and yet the having of it has never made him happy."

"That's just like the pompous old fart," Sarah's father grumbled under his breath.

"Is that all?" Sarah's mother broke in, her face a mask of incredulity. "Ten thousand dollars?"

Mr. Bryson nodded. "Yes. That is the amount stipulated in the will."

"Well, I never. It's spite, that's what it is. A bum could approach him on the street and be handed a dollar but he would deny his own flesh and blood."

"You're not his flesh and blood, so I don't see where you have reason to complain," Sarah's father said, stubbing out the cigar in an ashtray on the table. "I don't need his money, and I don't want it."

"Is there any mention of me in the will?" her mother addressed the attorney, her voice taking on a plaintive quality, which embarrassed Sarah.

"No, I'm afraid not, Mrs. Gallagher," said the lawyer.

Her mother then straightened herself and sniffed.

"Just as well. If you'll excuse me, gentlemen, Miss Gertrude, I will bid you adieu. I have a train to catch." She stood up.

"If you wait, dear, I have a carriage and driver and would be happy to take you to the station," said Aunt Gertrude.

"No thank you. I've had quite enough of this family already."

She gathered up her purse and mink collar and turned to Sarah.

"I will be moving to New York City in a fortnight. I've purchased a townhouse across from Gramercy Park. Come and have lunch with me one day soon."

"I would like that, mother," Sarah said. "Perhaps in a month or two."

Her mother nodded and, without another word, she left.

Everyone turned back to Mr. Bryson.

"I shall continue: I leave my sister Gertrude the sum of thirty thousand dollars and pray she does not spend it all on silly hats."

Sarah had to stifle a laugh, but then she saw that her aunt had taken the jest in good humor.

"I have always believed, Mr. Bryson, that a little of what you fancy does you good," her aunt said. "Isn't that so?"

"I must agree with you there, Miss Gertrude," the lawyer said with a hint of a smile. He continued reading.

"For my housekeeper, Phylida Hollins, I leave the sum of five thousand dollars. I leave a similar amount to my head gardener, Alphonse Garabino, who loves gladiolas as much as I do."

"To the Sailors' Rest Home of Key West, Florida, I leave the sum of forty thousand dollars. I only wish more people appreciated the hardships and dangers these brave men face each day transporting the necessities and luxuries of life across vast oceans so their fellow citizens might enjoy them."

The man with the eyebrows and ruddy complexion looked up toward the ceiling as if the deceased were in the room hovering just above their heads and said, "Mr. Gallagher, your generosity will soften the twilight years of many a weary mariner, and on behalf of the rest home, I thank ye."

The lawyer paused and looked at Sarah as if waiting for a signal to continue. Sarah felt all eyes upon her and she gave a slight nod.

"The remainder of my estate," the lawyer continued, "including all property real and otherwise, I leave to my granddaughter, Sarah Ann Gallagher. In my opinion, she is the best girl in the world who willingly shared with her

Papa the two most precious treasures we mortals possess: her time and her heart.

   Signed this day, August 12, 1886,
   Thomas Gladdius Gallagher."

Try as she might, Sarah could barely take in the magnitude of what had happened. She felt numb. Was it all to go to her: the money, properties, stocks and bonds, the businesses? She had expected a legacy, her grandfather had hinted at one, enough to pay her way through college and a little extra, perhaps enough to buy a small house. To her this had been in the realm of possibility. But the notion that she might inherit it all had never crossed her mind. This was partly because she had a superstitious streak, and to think about what she might gain from his death was to secretly wish it to happen. She would give all that she owned to have him back. The suffering of her heart was proof of that.

   Everyone was pushing back from the table getting ready to leave. Sarah caught her father looking at her. It wasn't the hard glare she knew only too well. No, it was as if he was trying to focus his eyes on her but having trouble, a mist filling the space between them. Then he shifted his gaze, stood up, and stepped closer to Mr. Bryson. Leaning over, he whispered something in the attorney's ear, who nodded, his eyes downcast. Her father then came over to her, his bearing formal.

   "You are a lucky girl, Sarah. I only wonder if you realize what having such a fortune entails. You will never know who your true friends are. Everyone will want something from you. You must learn to protect yourself or they will steal all that you have."

He then touched her on the head, like a priest giving a blessing, and left the room.

Sarah didn't know who the "they" were, those who would take her fortune from her. She felt tendrils of confusion reaching out to encircle her mind. Despite everything, she loved her father, but she also knew that he was lost to her, as was her quick-tempered, shallow mother.

"The good Lord may not allow me live much longer, my dear," said Aunt Gertrude retying her hat ribbon, "but as long as I am alive, you can count on me to be your friend and advisor."

"Thank you, Aunt Gertrude."

"I too will take my leave, if you don't mind," Mr. Smythe said. He handed Sarah a card with the name MR. TERRENCE SMYTHE printed on the front. "I do hope before you leave Key West, Miss Gallagher, you will honor us with a visit to the rest home. Without your grandfather's generous support and encouragement over the years, I doubt our organization would even exist."

"I would like very much to visit the home. Thank you."

Thus with one comment and another they all departed.

"Sarah, will you be returning to school?" Mr. Bryson asked when they were alone.

"I had planned to leave in the morning, but I'm not sure what to do now."

"Then I recommend you stay several more days at the very least so I can go over your grandfather's affairs with you."

"Yes, that would be very helpful. I'm afraid I have little experience managing money and property."

"We could meet tomorrow at your grandfather's house if that is not too difficult."

"No, I would like to visit the house. It is full of good memories." There was a pause and then Sarah spoke again.

"I know my grandfather trusted your judgment and discretion, Mr. Bryson, and I will do the same, if that is agreeable to you."

Bryson smiled. "If this old head can be of any service, it would be my pleasure to give you whatever advice I can.

"May I ask you a question then?"

"Certainly."

"What did my father say to you just before he left?"

The old man's eyes softened with affection as he looked at the young woman. How any father could treat a child like her with such indifference was beyond him.

"He told me he would not contest the will."

"Is that all?"

"Yes. The legacy is yours; I foresee no problems. Which reminds me, your grandfather placed in my keeping two items that he wanted me to give you after the reading of the will. They are in my office. If you will wait a moment, I will get them for you. There is a pitcher of sweet tea on the sideboard if you are thirsty."

The attorney left the room, and Sarah stood and paced. A school of thoughts darted first this way and that inside her mind and she noticed her hands were trembling. It took all her will power to adequately compose herself by the time Mr. Bryson returned.

He entered carrying a long narrow wooden box and a manila envelope. Sarah guessed the dimensions of the box to be three feet long, a foot wide, and eight inches deep. It was constructed of an exotic wood, ruby red with thin ribbons of black accentuating the grain. The finely engraved lock was of German silver.

The attorney placed the box on the table and handed the envelope to Sarah. It was sealed with red wax impressed with the letters *TG*.

"Your grandfather instructed me to tell you that the envelope contains a letter that he wishes for you to read alone in a quiet, private place. Only then should you open the box. The key for the box, I believe, is inside the envelope."

Sarah ran her fingers along the stiff envelope and felt the shape of a small key. Her natural curiosity battled an opposing, darker emotion. Was it fear? No, not fear, and yet there was an unaccountable reluctance to open the box.

"Mr. Bryson, would it be possible for you to keep this letter and box in your charge until after we have attended to my grandfather's estate? I'm at sixes and sevens and I would like to be more myself when I deal with them."

"Of course, my dear, I can imagine the inheritance has come as something of a shock."

"Yes, it has."

Sarah stepped out of the law office into bright sunshine, the azure sky swept clear of clouds. The young Mr. Hall accompanied her.

"May I hail you a carriage, Miss Gallagher?"

"No," she said, "I prefer to walk. I have a great deal to think about."

"Yes, well, the weather is most agreeable."

There was an awkward pause. A beer wagon rumbled by.

"Well, I have more work to do, so I will say goodbye."

He held out his hand and, as they shook, Sarah sensed the pain of his self-consciousness and was flattered.

He has such gentle eyes, she thought to herself, and wondered if he would assist Mr. Bryson on the morrow at her grandfather's house. She would welcome an opportunity to spend time with someone closer to her own age.

But then another thought intruded to poison this pleasant emotion. Did he know that she had just inherited a fortune? Of course he did. Was that the reason for his consideration?

He climbed three steps and opened the door to the office and turned for a parting glance, but Sarah swung away before their eyes could meet and hurried down the street. She realized her father's words were a curse; he wanted her to see the worst in everyone. A chill ran through her and, as she neared the bay, she made a decision. She would reject her father's suspicious ways. She would, instead, try and be like her grandfather, helping where help was needed and trusting in a fair but kindly judgment of people. She might be wanting in worldly sophistication, but she believed she was levelheaded and that should keep her out of any serious trouble.

Five days later, Sarah sat alone on the beach in front of her grandfather's house under the welcoming shade of a palm tree. A turquoise sea stretched out before her, the waves small and lazy, a bank of white clouds scudding along near the horizon, the remainder of the broad sky blue and untroubled. Resting on the white sand beside her was the wooden box. For days Sarah had wondered what it contained. Perhaps it was her grandmother's wedding dress, adorned with Seminole beadwork. Or the family silverware with the letter *G* engraved on each fork, spoon, and knife. The box might contain a collection of painted miniatures, a brass spyglass—it could be anything.

The last four days closeted with Mr. Bryson and his assistant, the helpful Mr. Hall, had exhausted her. They sifted through file cabinets filled with deeds and contracts, stock certificates and promissory notes, and even though Mr. Bryson did his best to ease her confusion she realized she needed to hire a secretary and an accountant. Returning to school was out of the question until next semester at the earliest. Perhaps she should offer Millie the position of secretary. Millie's father, a textile engineer, had died in a mill accident and she knew the family was struggling. A person could do good with money, she thought, but she might do harm as well.

She picked up the envelope that held the letter, lifting it to her nose to catch the familiar scent of her Papa. She then turned it over several times, rubbing the thick paper between her thumb and forefinger. She used a slender silver letter opener with an ivory handle that had belonged to her grandfather to break the seal and lift the flap. She pulled out a dozen sheets of thin paper and smiled at the tightly ordered penmanship she knew so well, no wasted flourishes, the words resting on an invisible line, straight as a ruler. How different her grandfather's script was to the lively stories he loved to tell, tales full of unexpected twists and turns and flights of imagination.

Tears began to push at the corners of her eyes, so she trained her gaze on a gull as it glided the length of the beach on outstretched wings before turning out over the water. Sarah then looked at the letter again and began to read.

Dearest Sarah,

My time to depart this world has come and I do so with a grateful heart, for I have known both friendship and love. I have also known wealth and the envy of others that comes with having wealth. How often did people ask, how could a young man with no family connections or prospects of any sort amass such riches? The answer, Sarah, is far more fantastic than anyone's heated imagination could have guessed and this is the story I will now impart to you, and to you alone.

My father and mother came to the United States from Ireland in 1814. They acquired thirty acres of rocky land in western Massachusetts near the town of Oxford. I was born there on May 9, 1821, the youngest of five children. Although my father worked hard, he was an unlucky farmer and we barely scratched a living from the land. He was, however, a fine musician. His choice of instrument was the violin, and he played on it the tunes he had heard growing up in Ireland, along with a smattering of tunes he picked up from a family of French Canadians who lived nearby. He seldom played his fiddle for money although we could have used it. Instead, he played for friends and family and for his own enjoyment in the evening when the work on the farm was done. We children would lie in our beds and listen to him as the winter wind beat upon the side of the house, or as summer rains danced upon the roof as if trying to keep time with the music.

Of the five children, I was the only one to express an interest in music. As long as I can remember, I had two great desires in life: to play the violin as well as my father and to go to sea in a grand ship under a mountain of crowded sail. As for the latter, I made model ships and sailed them on a pond near our house. I fashioned a marlin spike from the tip of a polished deer antler and learned to tie a variety of seaman's knots: the anchor hitch, bowline, sheet bend, shroud knot, rosebud stopper, and Turk's head. I scampered up tall pines barefoot pretending they were the masts of ships and I the faithful lookout. I even managed to acquire a book on navigation from a retired sea captain who lived in town, and at night I fell asleep with the book splayed open upon my lap as the candle burned down in its holder.

At the age of eleven, I built my first violin, a crude contraption with a carved chestnut neck attached to a cigar box and fitted with wire strings of varying thicknesses. If the truth be known, the violin made more noise than music but I was determined, so a year later my father traded a spring calf for a genuine German violin, which he presented to me on my thirteenth birthday. I suspect he did this as much to protect his ears as from any outpouring of paternal generosity. All the same, it was a superb instrument and it inspired me to redouble my efforts.

You might remember, Sarah, that I showed the violin to you once. I kept it in its black wooden case on the table in the library. Unfortunately, I suffered from arthritis later in life and was unable to play it for you. But it was a special instrument, and it saved my life on two separate occasions.

A seagull wheeled overhead and its cry brought Sarah back to the present moment. She recalled the violin resting inside its velvet-lined case like a baby in a cradle. Could such a delicate object save a man's life? She laid her hand on the top of the box wondering if it contained the violin. But then she remembered the reckoning of her grandfather's personal belongings that Mr. Bryson had given her. The violin was on the list. She shook her head and removed her hand; the violin was not in the box.

She picked up reading where she had left off.

The custom in that part of Massachusetts held that a person had to master a hundred tunes to be considered a

true fiddler, and that is the task I set myself. But as it was
for Joseph in the Old Testament, in the months and years
that followed the gift of the violin, my brothers increasingly
turned against me. They resented the fact that my father let
me stop work early so I could practice my music while they
were expected to continue toiling in the hot sun. This gave
rise to an atmosphere of hostility, and I looked forward to
the day when I would escape the farm and my brothers and
venture out to sea. When the morning of that day finally
arrived the sky was black with storm clouds and the smell of
rain was on the wind. This, however, mattered little to me
for I was young, just turned sixteen, and filled with the spirit
of adventure. My only possessions were a small valise and my
violin. On the lawn in front of our house I kissed my parents
goodbye, not knowing if I would ever see them again. My
mother gave me some wheat cakes and hard-boiled eggs for
the stagecoach journey to Boston, and after I arrived in the
city I stayed with an uncle while I sought a berth on a ship.
Eventually the captain of the *Arcadia*, who was much amused
by my fiddle playing, invited me to join his ship's company
as a cabin boy and I signed my name on the ship's register.
The *Arcadia* was bound for South America, her hold filled
with huge blocks of ice cut from the winter lakes of New
England. These blocks were surrounded by thick walls of
sawdust, which prevented the ice from melting before we
reached our destination below the equator.

The first month of my new employment sorely tried
my endurance and my shipmates took advantage of my
inexperience to pull many cruel pranks upon me. But I was
happy. It was the life I had so often dreamt of—at sea in a
proper Yankee clipper upon an endless ocean with my future
stretched out before me.

But alas, the *Arcadia* was an ill-fated ship, and disaster befell us off the island of Key West when a fierce gale drove us onto the Florida Reef, tearing the bottom out of our poor ship and drowning many of my fellow seamen. Miraculously, I was spared, kept afloat by my fiddle in its well-made wooden case, until a passing ship rescued me and took me to Key West.

I now found myself stranded amongst a strange people. They called themselves "wreckers," because they made their living salvaging and selling the cargo of the doomed ships dashed to pieces on the hidden reefs that ring their island. It was rumored that some islanders lit bonfires on shore to confuse the mariners at sea and draw them upon the reefs, but I never witnessed this despicable behavior myself. Perhaps it was merely an excuse given by captains to the owners of lost ships in hopes of absolving them of their own poor seamanship.

The survivors of *Arcadia* in time found berths in other ships, but I, an inexperienced youth, was not so fortunate.

Still, I had my violin and was able to feed myself by playing in the waterfront saloons. To the repertoire of Irish jigs and reels I had learned from my father, I added sea shanties and an assortment of hornpipes and quadrilles.

So it was that one night I met Largo Jack, as rough and salty a mariner as ever climbed a mast. I was playing for tips at the GREEN PARROT when Jack beckoned to me from his table in the corner. He was a frightening creature to behold, with a broad, white scar running diagonally from the top of his head across his forehead to his right ear, of which only half remained. Completing this tortured visage was a filthy leather patch covering his right eye, which he lifted like a gun port shutter on a man-of-war whenever he wished to emphasize a particular point he was making. Truly, Sarah, the effect of that milky-blue, lifeless orb gazing out of his rude face was enough to turn my blood to swamp water.

"You there, boy," Jack yelled to me after I had ignored his first mute summons. "Bring that fiddle over here and join old Jack for a swallow of rum. Barkeep, fetch me another bottle and cup. I feel the Devil's own thirst upon me."

The bartender, a heavy, slow-moving man with hair on his forearms as thick as seal pelts, shuffled his way to the table and set down a green bottle and a pewter cup.

"Here's your bottle, Largo Jack. And mind yourself. I'll stand no trouble tonight."

Jack tossed a silver coin onto the table and then hoisted the bottle to his lips and withdrew the cork with his remaining two yellowed teeth. Filling both cups, he set the bottle down and pushed one of them across the rough plank table toward me.

"Sit down now, sonny, and drink this. It'll take the hair off an oyster but it'll do you good. Do you by any chance play a tune called the *Sailor's Hornpipe?*"

I told him I did, as it was a favorite among the seagoing men.

"Then play it for old Jack, will ye, boy, while he drinks his rum."

I played the *Sailor's Hornpipe* several times through, and when I stopped he asked for another hornpipe called *Jacky Tar.* I followed that with a hornpipe of my own choosing called *The Boys of Bluehill.*

Well, time wore on and I sat there playing one tune after another for the old pirate. I call him a pirate, Sarah, because that is what I took him to be, and I was, in large measure, afraid of the man. But he meant me no harm. Instead, he was like a child, as delighted with the last tune as he was the first. Then, as the barkeep made to shutter the place, Jack beckoned me to come closer for he had something important to tell me. With some trepidation I drew near until I could smell the rum on his hot breath and the seaweed that rotted in his hair.

"Look here, sonny," he whispered, "I'm an old man with broken teeth, a bum leg, and only one lamp left burning on the starboard rail. I don't venture onto the water no more because when I do, I hear the Voices."

He shook his head slowly in a sorrowful way and his words confused me but I said nothing and he continued.

"I first went to sea when I was your age and my captains from first to last were pirates. Blackbeard and Thomas Tew and William Kidd, they were gone by then, and most of the Spanish gold, too. But there were still pickings: chests of silver coins, jewelry with the odd gemstone, and bolts of calico cloth. We didn't care. Anything we could sell, we took. What we couldn't sell we threw overboard for Neptune to bank."

He laughed, drained his cup, and filled it again.

"At the end I was with the Cuban pirate Captain Diabolito. Do you know what that means? Little devil, and God's truth the name suited him. Never have I known a creature that cared so little for man or beast, but only for what he could ransack and pillage. I could tell you stories, aye horrors, that no mother's son should ever hear, let alone be party to."

"Is he still alive?" I asked, having finally found my voice.

Largo Jack laughed. "No, they shot Captain Diabolito to death in the water after he was forced to abandoned his ship. The Americans trapped us just off the coast, and, as we tried to swim to safety, they shot us, one after another. I'm the only one who survived. They threw me in prison but I reformed and after a dozen years they set me free."

"How long ago did all this happen?"

Jack looked up as he ran his tongue over his pair of crooked teeth. "A long while ago, it's hard to reckon in years."

He jerked his face toward the door of the Green Parrot and called out. "Leave me alone. I'll not go with you."

I followed his gaze but saw no one, save the barkeep who was swabbing the floor with a heavy mop.

"Who are you talking to?" I asked.

"The Voices," Jack grumbled. "They've put such a mortal fright into me that I can barely keep from shaking."

He drained his cup in a single, long swallow.

"I didn't hear any voices." I said.

"Now you wouldn't, would you, because they belong to the poor, dead drowned sailors who we threw overboard for the sharks to eat, or blew to bloody pieces with our brass cannons. It's them that now calls to me from the deep."

"What do they want? The voices?"

"For me to join 'em. Aye, and it scares the bejesus out me, I don't mind telling you. So I stays on land now and I thinks that keeps me safe. Only, this very morning, see, I'm walking along the quay and I hear the Voices again. But now they say I ain't got long and they're waiting for me. So I'm sitting here in the Green Parrot brooding on how this might be my last night on God's good earth when I hear you playing your fiddle and, on my honor,—he banged his empty pewter cup on the table—I've never heard music such as you can make come out of that box of yours. Why, if I had a hundred silver pieces, I'd give them to you this very moment for entertaining me this lonely night and helping me remember them tunes I used to whistle as a young boy. But instead"—he leaned forward again—"I'm giving you this."

From inside his shirt he produced a yellowed and soiled sheet of thick paper that he spread out on the table, smoothing down the edges with his salt-cracked hands. In the yellow glare of dying candle, I saw a map of an island, with strange devices scrawled upon it in black India ink.

"Aye, it's a map, as you can see plain enough," Jack said, lowering his voice to whisper. "A treasure map, boy, that I've carried with me since back when I shipped with Captain Diabolito, the most dreaded buccaneer on the Spanish Main. That man made me do deeds that I burn to think of."

The barkeep yelled from across the room, "Drink up now, you two. I've got to close the place."

"Don't get your jib in a tangle, you son of a squid," Jack growled back at him and then he dropped his voice again.

"So listen to what I'm telling you. There's a treasure, a mighty great treasure, and you can have it for yourself if you're bold enough, and if you can play your fiddle as if your very life depends on it."

"What kind of treasure? Where is it?" I asked.

"Here!" He stabbed the map with his forefinger shaking the table. "On Kingfisher Island, just sixty sea miles from where we sit. A chest full of gold coins and silver bars thick as loaves of bread. And there are precious jewels, mind you, a fair trove of rubies, diamonds, and sapphires."

Then lowering his voice even more, he said, "But there's the *Guardian* to reckon with. Aye, there's always a guardian. That's the pirates' way of doing things, don't you know."

I asked him what a guardian was and he snorted.

"It's a ghost, boy, a bloody, friggin' ghost who swings a cutlass in his bony hand as sharp as a gentleman's razor. See, it's like this: a pirate captain is forced to bury his treasure from time to time to keep the weight of it from sinking his ship. So he has his men row the treasure ashore on a moonlit night to some remote island where they dig a deep hole in the sandy soil. Then, after the treasure's been lowered into the ground, the captain kills one of his own men, aye in cold blood, and throws the corpse into the hole with the treasure, commanding the dead seaman's spirit to watch over the treasure until the captain returns for it. And murdered or not, the man's ghost must do as he is ordered because he's sworn a blood oath of obedience to his pirate captain, an oath that follows him into the next world."

"Did Captain Diabolito ever return for his treasure?"

"Nay, or why would Largo Jack be holding on to this here map all these years? You see, after they released me from prison I drifted from port to port, like jetsam pushed here and there by the wind and currents. But all the time I was thinking about Diabolito's treasure and how I might go and dig it up. The desire was like a splinter jammed under my thumbnail or a shred of meat stuck in my teeth; it gave me no rest. But then I was afraid, wasn't I, of me old shipmate Jonesy. It be his ghost that's protecting Diabolito's treasure, until the end of time."

The barman dropped a shutter with a bang that made me jump. Jack paid it no mind.

"But there *is* a way to get that treasure. You see, I've been studying on it. Jonesy, he wasn't a bad sort really, as far as pirates go. And my, but how he loved to dance. On my oath, many's the time he'd entertain us weary jack tars by the light of the moon, scampering back and forth across the deck of our ship like a monkey, to the music of the squeezebox or fife.

"Tonight you played some of the very tunes he liked to dance to aboard ship and I says to myself, Jack, that be the very way to get the treasure. Only I'm too old and too near my end to make the journey now. So I'm giving you the treasure as a gift, and good luck to you."

As you can imagine, Sarah, my head swam from both the rum and the pirate's strange tale.

"But if I find the place where the treasure is buried, and it is still there, will I have to deal with Jonesy's ghost?"

"Aye, you will, boy, but that's where the fiddling comes in," Jack replied, nodding his head by way of urging me to understand. "Look, here's what you do. Wait until the full moon before you go to the place marked on the map. Go alone and bring with you a hunk of meat. Jonesy favored mutton, but if you can't find mutton, I allow beef or pork will do. Build up a fire and put the meat on a spit and hang it over the fire to roast. Do this just as the sun is setting, and, as it gets dark and the moon comes up and the smell of the meat is all about the place, then you'll see Jonesy. He'll sort of rise up from the ground, like a vapor. But don't be fooled; he'll be real enough."

Then it struck me and I blurted out, "My God, you've done this! You've seen Jonesy's ghost, haven't you?"

A grimace wracked Largo Jack's features as if the memory caused him physical pain.

"Aye, I saw the restless shade and before I knew it, he was after me, and me running for me life. Lookie here."

He rolled up his right shirtsleeve to reveal a broad scar that reached from his elbow to his wrist.

"Jonesy caught me there with his accursed cutlass, blast

him, and very nearly sliced off me arm as I dove into the skiff."

He rolled his sleeve back down.

"So I never went back to Kingfisher Island again, damn his hide."

He drained his cup and wiped his lips and mustache with the back of his hand.

"But you see, you've got your fiddle and I be thinking that be the trick. If you can start Jonesy dancing, see, instead of swinging his cutlass about, and if you can keep him dancing long enough, why, sure as creation, the treasure will be yours."

"But how long would I have to keep him dancing?"

"Until you've worn him out. But Jonesy was a mighty dancer when the spirit was in him. I've known him to dance the night away more than once. So there is a risk, but ain't that what life is all about, one grand risk after another, before death comes and takes your breath away?

The barman dropped the last of the storm shutters. Jack folded up the map and handed it to me.

"Here. Take it. May it bring you more luck than it's brought me, or Jonesy, come to think of it. It's time I be shoving off for me hammock."

"But how do I get to Kingfisher Island?" I asked.

"Find an old salt called Scully. He's a Scotsman who owns a fishing boat called the *Primrose*. He's a rough old oyster on the outside but, inside, a rare pearl of a shipmate. There's precious few on these islands I would trust as I do Scully. He'll stand the watch, no matter how strong the gale."

I had more questions, many more, but as we made our way out into the dark Key West night, I could see Jack's mind had turned in on itself and he walked away without another word. I never saw the old pirate again, and, for all I know he joined those Voices that called to him from their watery graves.

As for myself, I wandered the streets of Key West until the early hours of the morning. Only then did I return to my small room at the boarding house, where I fell into a fitful sleep haunted by dark, silent shapes flitting among the mangroves in the moonlight. My Yankee sense tried to convince me that Largo Jack was nothing but an incorrigible old liar, his brain pickled by too much rum and unbridled imagination. He had spun me a true sailor's yarn, and, like the young fool I was, I had let him run on until the cost of the drinks came out of my pocket, not his. And yet for the next two days, his words continued to nag me and I found myself pulling out the old map at odd moments to study the inscriptions scrawled upon it.

By the third day, I realized I would have no peace until I played the game to its end. Thus I began patrolling the wharves and docks asking where I might find a ship called the *Primrose* and Scully, her captain. Then one day I spied an old sailor perched on a barrel next to a sloop mending his fishing nets and singing a lively sea shanty.

Since we sailed from Plymouth Sound
Four years gone or nigh, Jack,
Was there ever chummies now,
Such as you and I, Jack?

Long we've tossed to the rolling main,
Now we're safe ashore, Jack.
Don't forget your old shipmate,
Faldd raldee raldee raldee rye-eye-doe!

Oftentimes have we laid out,
Toil nor danger fearing.
Tugging out the flapping sail,
To the weather earring.

Long we've tossed to the rolling main,
Now we're safe ashore, Jack.
Don't forget your old shipmate,
Faldd raldee raldee raldee rye-eye-doe!

But the best of friends must part,
Fair or foul the weather,
Hand your flipper for a shake,
Now a drink together.

Long we've tossed to the rolling main,
Now we're safe ashore, Jack.
Don't forget your old shipmate,
Faldd raldee raldee raldee rye-eye-doe!

When he finished his ditty, he yelled to another jack tar who was busy swabbing the foredeck of the sloop. "Throw me your marlinspike, Hal. Me nets are jumbled up like Medusa's hair."

With a clunk, the marlinspike landed on the dock at the sailor's feet. I approached and spoke.

"Pardon me, I'm looking for a sailor named Scully."

"And what would you be wanting with Scully, laddie?"

"I was told he was an honest man who could take me to Kingfisher Island."

The sailor let out a harsh laugh like that of a hungry seabird. "You hear that, Bert?" he turned and yelled. "The boy says Scully's an *honest* man."

Then he turned and a fixed me with a stare and said, "Look, laddie, there's many won't walk down a dark alley with old Scully, let alone cast off to sea with him.

"But Largo Jack told me to find him, and him alone."

The suspicious eyes narrowed even more to a look of keen interest. "You've seen Largo Jack then? When? Where? Speak!"

"Three—no, four nights ago down at the GREEN PARROT."

"You wouldn't be fibbing me, would you now, laddie? I've no use for jokers. Why, I'd throw you in the harbor if I thought you were playing the skylark with me."

"No, sir, I wouldn't."

"Wouldn't what?"

"Play the skylark, as you say. I did see Largo Jack, well, a man who called himself Largo Jack, and he told me to find a sailor named Scully."

"What did he look like then? Describe him for me and be quick about it."

"Well, he was about my height, but heavier set. He had one good eye, and a patch over the other."

"Argh, that describes most of the old pelicans roosting about the town," said the old sailor with spit of disgust. "Don't you know it cures the seasickness to have only one eye?"

"And he had a scar on his forehead, here," I said pointing to my own forehead, "that ran down to his ear. And he had another on his right forearm, from the elbow to his wrist."

Slapping his knee, the sailor yelped, "So Jack's washed ashore in Key West in the end. Well, I'll be keelhauled! I'm the Scully you're a looking for." He held out his hand for me to shake while whispering so none but me could hear, "You've got to be careful around here letting out who knows who, if you get my drift. I was Jack's tie-mate for many a year until he got the spooks and went and disappeared on me. Been in some tough scraps together, old Jack and me. Did he tell you that he once saved my life? No? Well, he did, but that's a long tale."

He squinted as the memory passed through him and he let out a wistful sigh, "Largo Jack, by my stars. I've only caught rumors of him over the years and figured he'd shoved off to Fiddler's Green long before now."

"Where is Fiddler's Green?" I asked.

"Why, you are dry behind the ears, laddie. Fiddler's Green is where all sailors go when we ship out with Captain Death. They say it's a place where you can have all the rum and tobacco you crave, and there's always fiddlers playing and the grandest dancing that ever was. So now, why did Largo Jack send you to find me?"

"I need a boat and someone to take me to Kingfisher Island."

"But what would you be wanting with Kingfisher Island? There's naught there but scrub mangrove and mosquitoes."

"I need to look for something, and if I find it I'll pay you handsomely for your troubles."

"Handsomely, you say?" he said and laughed. "Look, laddie, it'll take us two days or more to sail to Kingfisher Island and then three days to get back, provided we have the wind. That's five full days of sailing, not counting how long it'll take you to find whatever it is you're looking for. Now I could spend those five days fishing and make as much as twenty-five dollars. So if you were to *give* me twenty-five dollars, I might agree to take you to Kingfisher Island."

"But I don't have anywhere near that much money," I said.

"How much money do you have, then?"

"I only have two dollars, from playing my fiddle."

"Aye, that's what I thought," he said taking up the marlinspike and shoving it through a tangle in his net. "Leave me to get back to my work."

I was surprised by the sound of my own voice as I blurted out, "But I own a jim-dandy violin, and it comes with a fine wood case and bow."

"And what's that to me?" Scully said without looking up from his work. "I don't play the fiddle and I'm not keen to learn how."

"But you could sell it. If you take me to the island and I don't find what I'm looking for and can't pay you, then you can sell the violin. It's worth more than twenty-five dollars."

He looked up then. "You *are* in a lather to make the voyage, that's plain to see. And if you do find what you're looking for, what then?"

"I'll pay you a hundred dollars."

"A hundred dollars?" Scully shook his head and pursed his lips. "No, laddie, you will pay me a twentieth share of what you find, and we'll call it square. Will you shake on it?"

He spit in the palm of his calloused hand and held it out. I paused and tried to calculate what a twentieth part of a great treasure was worth. I noticed Scully studying me, his hand still outstretched.

Then I laughed at my foolishness. Without Scully there would never be a treasure. I spit and shook and the bargain was fixed.

We waited for the fifteenth of the month to make our voyage to Kingfisher Island, which was two days before the full moon. The weather was agreeable and Scully proved himself an able navigator. He had a way of talking about the sea that helped me see it with new eyes and I was glad for his cheerful talk, for dread was settling over me like a creeping fog the further south and east we sailed. Over and over again I reproached myself for taking Largo Jack at his word. I feared I would soon be parted from my cherished violin, the only means I had of securing a living. But there were other moments when I felt the opposite, that what the old pirate had told me *was* true. And with these thoughts churning like dark water inside my mind, it was a long two days' sail to Kingfisher Island.

"There she is, laddie!" Scully crowed when Kingfisher Island came up out of the sea to greet us. "As lonely and forgotten a bit of ground as you will find in this watery part of the world. I've been meaning to ask you. What do you have stowed in the sack? Ever since our first day out, I've been smelling it."

"It's a haunch of salted mutton," I told him, hoping more questions would not follow.

"Then tell old Scully what do you plan to do with the meat."

"I'm going to cook it."

"But you have enough there to feed twenty men."

"It's for the smell. I need the smell of cooked meat to find what I'm looking for."

"Would that be following Jack's instructions?"

"Yes, it is what he told me to do."

"Aye, it figures. Jack had his strange ways, and many there were who laughed at him, but not me. No, I always reckoned he had the *sight*."

"What *sight*?" I asked.

Scully lowered his voice for no reason I could discern; it was just the two of us in a wilderness of seawater. "The second sight, laddie. Have ye never heard tell of it? Me granny had it. She could tell when folks were coming to visit long before they hove into sight. Could tell if a lassie, heavy with child, was going to deliver a wee boy or girl, just by looking. It's in the blood. There's some who have it, and most who don't. Best trust what old Jack told you. Now watch yourself as I come about."

We found a sheltered inlet to drop anchor and from there Scully rowed me to the beach in a skiff.

"I'll have me a bit of rest here and you go on about your business," Scully said, tying the skiff to a bleached drift log. He then pulled his pistol from his belt and offered it to me.

"Just in case, laddie."

But I knew the weapon would be of no use to me and shook my head.

Scully shrugged and pushed it back in under his belt.

Even though Largo Jack had told me to go alone, I desperately wanted Scully to accompany me, for I was truly frightened of what I might find.

"I'm looking for a treasure," I blurted out. I expected a look of astonishment to appear on the old mariner's sunburned face but instead he just laughed.

"I guessed as much. With Jack it was always about booty."

"Then you'll come with me? I'll share the treasure with you, fifty-fifty."

At that the Scotsman laughed again. "Look, laddie. You've got old Scully pegged wrong. I've no desire for great heaps of dead men's gold. It's sure to bring me bad luck and enemies. Or trouble with the bottle. What did Jack tell you to do?"

"He told me to go alone," I answered.

"And why bring the mutton?"

"It's for the ghost."

"For the *ghost*, you say?" From his tone of voice and the way he raised his eyebrow I couldn't tell if he believed this or was making fun of me. Either way, I felt foolish, so I tied the sack to the handle of the shovel I had brought and lifted them unto my shoulder. The violin case was fitted with a leather strap so I could carry it strung across my back. Rigged up in this fashion, and with the map to direct me, I set off, leaving Scully leaning against a coconut tree, contentedly smoking his pipe.

It took me more than an hour to reach the place marked on the map, which was halfway across the small island, because I had to fight my way through thick underbrush most of the way. It was hot, exhausting work, and the back of my hands bled in numerous places where the sharp ends of branches had torn my skin. And I will tell you, my dear Sarah, I cursed myself more than once for being such a dunce. But finally, just before sunset, I came to a clearing. To my left was a mosquito-infested pond, to my right a pair of ancient palm trees. Consulting the map, I determined I had found the clearing where Captain Diabolito's gold was buried. I placed my burdens on the sandy ground and scavenged bits of dry wood with which to build a fire. I had some squares of paper and a dozen Lucifers wrapped in oilcloth tucked into my belt and I soon had a lively blaze. The day had been warm and yet there was an unnatural chill about the place and all I could think about was Jonesy's brutal murder. How was it done? Bloody images flooded into my mind unbidden. Did Captain Diabolito waste powder and lead on the unfortunate seaman or did he run him through with his cutlass? Did Jonesy suspect that he was the one chosen to guard the treasure or was he struck down unawares from behind? That would be Diabolito's way, I imagined. He was known to fly a counterfeit flag so as to draw near his prey—a Union Jack for England, the Le Drapeau Tricolore for France, the Stars and Stripes for the United States. Only when it was too late to resist would the victim see the dreaded skull and crossbones go flapping up the main mast. How that sight must have struck terror into the hearts of even the bravest men.

I jammed two forked branches into the sand on opposite sides of the fire and pulled the mutton from the sack and ran a stick through it. I then suspended the meat over the flames, and it wasn't long until drops of grease began dripping into the fire, making it sputter and causing fingers of flame to lick upwards and blacken the meat. I was so intent on my work that I didn't notice the darkness of night close in about me. In the east, the full moon was rising and all about me the air was heavy with the pungent aroma of roasting meat. My legs ached with fatigue, but I feared to sit, squatting instead next to my open fiddle case so I could run at a moment's notice if I had to. Sweat from fear and the heat of the fire drenched my shirt and mosquitoes dodged the wood smoke to attack me, but I paid them no mind.

Then I saw him. He rose slowly out of the sand not ten feet from where I crouched. First to appear was his head, then his neck, his arms, and his torso. At last there appeared his legs and feet. I gaped, dumbfounded, because, even though I knew Jonesy was a spirit, I had expected him to appear much as he had in life, dressed in the pliant flesh and flowing hair of the human form. But now I saw the error in my thinking, for standing before me was a creature stripped clean of skin and muscle, of sinew and organ. He was nothing but a collection of bones in the approximation of a man, with each bone bleached white as a sand dollar. I nearly swooned as I gazed upon that skull sporting its hideous death grin, but then the flash of a seaman's cutlass in the moonlight brought me to my senses. The skellybones held the weapon in his left hand and swung it in a mad arc above his head as he stepped toward me, the steel bright and untarnished despite having lain buried for so many years.

My instinct, of course, Sarah, was to bolt, but I earnestly believe, had I done so, the skellybones would have cut me down before I had reached the edge of the clearing. So instead, I thrust my fiddle under my chin and began to play *Soldier's Joy*, the first tune I learned as boy, and the only one that came to mind in that desperate moment.

I played through the first part of the tune and to my tremendous relief, I saw Jonesy check his step and cant his head to the side on its bony axis, as if listening to something long forgotten. He stood frozen like that for a dozen heartbeats. Then I noticed his right foot begin to pat the sand. Up and down, up and down, the bony foot moved to the tempo of the music. His bony legs then commenced to bend at the knee joints so that he took on the posture common to men who have spent many years at sea upon a rolling deck. With a jolt of inner knowing, I changed keys and began playing *Sailor's Hornpipe*, the tune I had played for Largo Jack back in the GREEN PARROT. That was all it took. Still clutching the cutlass on high, the skellybones began to step across the sand in the manner of a proper hornpipe, his dry bones rattling in the still night air.

It was a comical sight, Sarah: the meat sizzling on the spit, the shadows cast by the flickering fire, and a skeleton capering about to the notes of a fiddle on a deserted island. But I knew only one emotion: terror. It was a terror born out of the certainty that should I falter the least bit, or should the ghost suddenly grow bored with the tune I was playing, he would be upon me in an instant to cleave my head from my shoulders with a single swift stroke of his cutlass! And so I played for my very life, and, as I moved on from tune to tune, Jonesy adapted his steps to each subtle change of rhythm and tempo. This ghost certainly loved to prance; it was, forgive me for saying this, Sarah, in his bones.

Back home in Massachusetts I often played for contra dances and those were lengthy affairs, each couple moving in elaborate figures all the way up the hall and then down again, but never had I played as I did that night. My fingers ached, the muscles in my bowing arm throbbed from the constant sawing across the strings, and my neck and chin grew so stiff I feared, should I survive, I would be deformed, locked in that unnatural position for the rest of my life. This was only one of a host of dark fears to assail me that night. What if a string broke? What if the bow used up its portion of rosin and began skipping across the strings without making a sound? I knew I must not stop, even for a heartbeat, without paying dearly.

And whenever I was near to breaking, I would gaze upon my tormenter and, as if to taunt me, he would fly into fits of wild abandon, raking the hilt of his heavy cutlass up and down the bones of his rib cage, producing a queer, percussive racket to accompany my melodies.

On and on it went. I lost all track of the time. How long would it take until the creature tired of his crazy dance and left me in peace? What memory had these bones retained of the flesh and blood life they had once supported: the tang of the salt sea in the nostrils, the gay notes of the concertina in the ears, the brush of the cool night breeze upon the cheeks, the starlight above the quarterdeck in the eyes, the caress of sweet rum upon the tongue? How he must have relished the days when the warm blood flowed in his veins and he sailed the main with his pirate companions, a law unto themselves and feared by one and all.

But then my thoughts returned to my own plight. I grew so weary I could barely stand. My body cried out for me to stop. I struggled to think of new tunes to play. Would I remember their notes without stumbling? Here in front of me was my harshest critic. But God be praised, Sarah, that man did love to dance!

When the change began to occur I cannot say, so fixed was I upon the music. But the skellybones, little by little, began to lose track of the tempo, a bony step late on the downbeat, the arm, holding the cutlass, falling more and more often to his side. Yes, I saw that my tormentor of the long night was at last tiring. The realization gave me renewed hope and energy. I picked up the tempo, even though the effort shot stabbing pains up and down my arm. Jonesy's motions grew jerky; the bravado was gone and desperation had taken hold. At long last, the cutlass dropped from his bony fingers and stuck upright in the sand. And still I played, the ghost careening off in large circles like a drunkard, his bony legs wobbling. I noticed then that the fire had burned down to coals, its service for the eyes overtaken by the first gray light of dawn. I had played the night away. The dancer then dropped to his knees at the very place where he had first appeared, and, with a final jerk of his arm, fell over on his side and lay motionless. I lifted the bow from the strings and lowered the fiddle from my chin. My ears rang in the sudden silence. A stiff wind kicked up. It blew across the poor creature's bones and they began to dissolve, blowing away like fine sand. In a moment he was gone and I wished him eternal peace.

What took place next was as Largo Jack had predicted. At the spot where the skellybones fell, I dug down into the sand, and soon my shovel scraped something hard. I dug more and uncovered a great leather bound sea chest. Casting the shovel aside, I jumped into the hole. I tried to lift the chest but it was too heavy. Besides, I could barely lift my arms from their long night's exertion. Already the day was growing warm and I made my way back to Scully, who had built a small fire and was boiling coffee.

"I'm glad to see you're still alive," he said with a welcoming smile.

"That I am. And rich as Midas. I found the treasure." I was a crowing rooster.

"And the ghost?"

That pulled the wind from my sails and I shook my head to drive away the memory.

"He is no more," was all I said, and Scully let it be.

"But I need your help," I said. "I cannot lift the treasure chest. It is large and heavy."

"Is there only one chest?"

The question caught me by surprise. "I think so. I stopped digging when I found it."

"Pirates bury treasure because of its weight. There could more than one chest. Come, let's have a look."

Scully remained calm, even after we had uncovered three more chests, which struck me as unnatural.

In the chests we found some gold, but mostly we found silver coins, gem-encrusted jewelry, and sterling tableware. And there were rolls of calico, valuable spices, and even a Bible whose cover was made of embossed silver. It took a great deal of effort but we carried the treasure to our little skiff that was pulled up onto the beach.

"We can't take it all at once," Scully said, "or the weight will send *us* to the bottom. We'll have to make numerous trips."

And here, I am ashamed to say, Sarah, I grew fearful that, once the treasure was onboard Scully's ship and we were at sea, he would murder me and throw my body overboard. What was there to stop him? And yet to abandon the treasure after all I had been through, this I could not do. So I told myself that I must trust him. We stowed the treasure in the hold and set sail for home. The weather was kind and as we approached Key West, Scully cautioned me on how to keep the treasure secret.

"Now, laddie, if there's one thing I've learned in life, it's not the *getting* of something that's as hard as the *keeping* of it. But I will help you as best I can. I know a hidden cove where no one goes. We'll put in there and unload the treasure. We'll dig a pit and cover the treasure with sand and palm leaves. Then you can transport the treasure back to your boarding house or some other place a bit at a time so no one notices. You've got a young, strong body, laddie, but let's hope you've got an old man's head on your shoulders."

That then, Sarah, is the story. Scully, the rare man that he was, proved true to his word. He took only a twentieth of the treasure, even though I urged him to take more. It took us three voyages in all to return the treasure to Key West and more than a year for me to dispose of the treasure without raising suspicion. The money I received from the sale of these items I invested, and, with Mr. Bryson's help and advice, I prospered.

I never saw Largo Jack again. Scully bought a house in town and a new fishing boat and lived out his years free from want. He died long before you were born, but I would have liked for you to have met him.

You are now the mistress of a great fortune. Although you are young, I believe you have the gift of sense and will not squander it. Remember, my dear, what Scully taught me when I was your age: it is not the getting that is difficult, it is the keeping of it. Be wise. Be kind. And above all, be happy.

Your loving Papa

Sarah folded the letter and slipped it back into the envelope. To think that her grandfather had really survived such an ordeal filled her with wonder, but a wonder tinged with the dread of the unknown. She considered the wooden box. Did it contain the last of Diabolito's stolen treasure: a jeweled goblet to grace a bishop's altar or perhaps a sack of Spanish doubloons? No, she told herself, not treasure. Knowing her grandfather, it would be something to prove beyond a doubt that this one story, at least, was true. Smiling with the realization of what was inside the box, she fitted the key into the lock, turned it, and lifted the lid. And there before her, gleaming bright in the Florida sunshine, without blemish of rust or age, was her grandfather's final gift to her: the skellybones's cutlass.

FORGET-ME-NOT

"I've always said Emma was big-hearted," whispered the tall woman under the wide brimmed hat to the shorter woman standing next to her. "I mean, the way she went and married Walter, even after that terrible accident; few women would have done a thing like that."

The shorter woman nodded, encouraging the born talker to continue.

"Why, she could have broken off the engagement and not a soul in Phelp's Mill would have uttered a word against her."

"He needed looking after," the shorter woman said.

"I'll say he did, but that's work for a hired girl, not a young wife."

The tall woman sighed and gazed into the distance. "But I reckon Emmie had her reasons."

Her companion was about to say it was because of love but was hushed by the preacher, who opened his carrying-around Bible and cleared his throat.

"My brothers and sisters in Christ. We are gathered here today in the sight of God to bid farewell to Emma Hendricks.

"Let us pray: The Lord is my shepherd; I shall not want. He makes me lie down in green pastures . . ."

Thus was Aunt Emma laid to rest in a small country cemetery under the leafy branches of a hundred-year old sugar maple, while cicadas sang in the summer grass.

Walter sat in his wheelchair at the edge of the grave with a bouquet of flowers that he had cut that morning in the garden on his lap. He laid them on the top of the coffin after the prayer was finished and before Emma was lowered into the dark ground to await the Day of Judgment. His features betrayed no trace of the emotions roiling him inside, reluctant to say goodbye to his best friend and constant companion, his comforter and confessor.

Circling the grave were several dozen men and women. Most came from the surrounding farms, but a few, like Hank Ogren, were from town. Hank was president of the FARMERS TRUST BANK and he had driven out to Phelp's Mill in his brand new 1934 ESSEX TERRAPLANE. Standing next to Hank was Judge Kyle Mannington and his wife Elsie. It didn't matter who you asked, rich or poor, Aunt Emma was loved and respected and would be missed.

Emma Starr met Walter Hendricks at a dance in 1890 when she was twenty years old. Walter was a strong, good-looking boy with bright blue eyes and an easy laugh. Two months later they got engaged. But then Walter had his accident. He was skidding saw logs out of the woods, driving a team of Percherons, when a log broke loose and rolled down on top of him, crushing both his legs. That he survived the accident at all was considered something of a miracle. He nearly bled to death in the back of Bob Durbin's wagon on the way to Doc Mooney's. The old doc did his best to save the legs, but when gangrene set in several days later, he was forced to amputate, removing each leg just above the knee.

Emma stayed by Walter's side throughout this horrific ordeal, even though he repeatedly offered to release her from her promise to be his wife.

"For better or for worse," she told him whenever the subject came up, "that's what the vows say."

"But you haven't said the vows and I'm now a broken man, Emmie. I can't give you the life you deserve."

"The body is broken, not the man. We'll manage somehow. God will watch over us."

So they were married. Walter's father bought them a house as a wedding present. It came with a large vegetable garden and four cleared acres, enough for a brood of chickens and a mob of pigs.

Emma's family did their part as well. Her father was a county commissioner, and, when the position of postmaster for Phelp's Mill came open, he saw to it that his new son-in-law got the job. Emma and Walter turned the front room of their house into a combination post office and general store and settled into their new life together, the days coming like heartbeats, one after another.

Now it is said that misfortune and blessing are two buckets drawn from the same well, and so it was for Walter. Before the accident he was an active man, a hard worker and a good dancer. Now, confined to a wheelchair, he often suffered bouts of depression, which worried Emma, so she did what she could to cheer him up.

On their second Christmas together she handed him a large box wrapped in brown paper and a red silk ribbon.

"What's in the box, Emmie?" Walter asked. "It's half as big as you."

"Well, why not open it and find out."

He untied the ribbon and tore the paper away to reveal a leather-covered violin case. Lifting the lid, he found a beautiful violin, with a bow made from Brazilwood and wrapped with silver wire.

"Everett got it off a Frenchman in Baltimore," Emma said.

Everett was her older brother—all five of her siblings had names that started with the letter E—and Everett worked as a superintendent for the railroad.

"The Frenchie was a sailor," Emma continued the story. "He got tangled up with the law and needed cash money quick, and Everett came away with the fiddle."

"What did it cost him?"

"He wouldn't say but he allowed it would cost me a half-dozen eggs a week for a year." Emma laughed and Walter couldn't tell if she was joking or not.

"No, really," he said. "This violin must have cost plenty."

"Stop fretting about money for once," Emma scolded. "Flip it over and look at the back. Everett says it's made with flame maple. Hold it up to the light. See? Don't it look just like fire?"

"It sure is nice, Emmie."

"Didn't you tell me once that when you were a boy you wanted to learn to play the fiddle?"

"I did, but my mother wouldn't allow one in the house.

"Why in the world not?"

"Because she's a Baptist and the fiddle is used for dancing and such carrying on."

"But your Uncle Luke played the fiddle. And what about your father's cousin over in Kentucky? What's his name? Doesn't he play the fiddle?"

"Uncle Ambrose did, until he had a stroke."

"Well then, maybe music-making is in your blood."

"But won't me learning to play this thing drive you away? It's sure to sound like a sack full of scalded cats."

"I can stand it if it keeps you from moping."

And it turned out that Emma was right about music being in Walter's blood. In practically no time he could play his way through *Jump Jim Crow* and *West Fork Girls* and *Goin' Down to Georgia-O.* He spent hours each day practicing and learning little tricks like plunking the E string with his pinkie finger while playing *Too Young To Marry*, or bouncing his bow from string to string as he played *Drunken Hiccups.* The fiddle became a source of great pleasure for him and Emma both. Emma loved to garden and she made the rows extra wide so Walter could keep her company in his wheelchair. He liked to play his fiddle for her while she hoed corn and picked beans. Sometimes Emma sang along with the tunes, a practice called "lilting" that she had picked up from her Irish grandfather.

One bright blue spring day after they had been married a score of years, a professional photographer showed up at the store. He drove a two-horse wagon with a large enclosed box on the back, the kind medicine show pitchmen traveled the country with. But instead of bottles of HOSTETTER'S CELEBRATED STOMACH BITTERS and boxes of MYALTOE CORN AND BUNION PLASTERS containing "20% cannabis indica," his wagon contained box cameras, gangly tripods, and magnesium flash pans. It also served as his darkroom for developing his pictures.

"My name is Artemus Browne," the man introduced himself to Walter who was minding the store. "I was hoping you could tell me if anyone hereabouts might be interested in having their portraits taken. I've been trained by some of the best photographers in Philadelphia and New York and know my business, if I do say so myself."

He was a short, compact man with a chinstrap beard, and a hefty gold watch chain that dangled from one vest pocket to another. There was something about the way he talked that made Walter grin.

"The Mortenson's are a vain bunch," Walter told him. "They live a ways up Finger Lick."

"You don't have to be vain to want to have your picture taken," the man said.

"You're right there," Walter said and then an idea popped into his head. "I'll tell you what. If I find you some folks willing to pay to have their pictures made, would you give me a discount on a photograph of my wife?"

"That seems fair to me. We've all got to help each other if we hope to get through this troublesome world without getting too banged up."

"But I've got to warn you. My wife's so pretty she might break your camera."

"No worry there, mister," the man said with a laugh. "I have a special lens for extra pretty women."

Emma, sorting mail, overheard this exchange and turned her face away so the stranger wouldn't see her blush. Walter can be so danged sweet, she thought to herself. It made up for all the hard work and looking after.

Several days later, Mr. Browne stopped by the store with Emma's photograph and to say goodbye. He had photographed eleven families, a team of horses, a prize-

winning hog, and a corpse, this last belonging to Ned
Barbour, who died of a busted appendix.

The photograph made Walter as happy as a dog wagging
two tails, and he ordered an oval gilt frame from a company
in Cincinnati. When it came, he hung Emma's photograph
with pride on their sitting room wall.

Now Emma was gone and Walter was an old man on his
own. He decided to keep the store and post office going,
but he was lonely, and often played his fiddle late into night
when he couldn't sleep.

About this time, the PENNAFLEX COMPANY began work
on a natural gas pipeline that would snake its way through
the north end of the county. The foreman of the PENNAFLEX
crew was an accomplished fiddler named Jimmy Reeves.
On Saturday nights he would show up at local dance halls
decked out in custom-made alligator-skin boots, a white
satin shirt with snap buttons, and a pearl gray Stetson.

"You boys mind if I join in?" he would ask the band leader,
and more times than not the leader would invite him up on
stage and he would play with such force that the notes fairly
jumped out of his fiddle. Of course, this excited the dancers
and they twirled faster and kicked their heels up higher, and
soon Reeves would be right up in front, closest one to the
microphone, crowding the other fiddlers off to the side.

And that is exactly how the foreman wanted it. He liked
being top dog with his fiddle tucked tight and neat under his
chin and all the pretty girls giving him the eye.

One night Reeves showed up at a dance at a Disciples of
Christ Church at the mouth of Willow Run, not far from
Phelp's Mill. Walter Hendricks was the lead fiddler that
night and they had an extra microphone set low so he could

play while seated in his wheelchair. Reeves had never seen such an arrangement before, and he held back and listened for a while. Bold as he was, Reeves was impressed by the old man's style of fiddling. He was also captivated by the sound of Walter's violin, the one Emma's brother purchased from the Frenchman. To Reeves' ear it had an exceptionally sweet tone, yet it was loud enough to be heard over the other instruments, even the piano. He realized it was the fiddle he had been looking for all his life.

"Would you mind if I gave your fiddle a try?" he said to Walter while the band was taking a break and the dancers had stepped outside to cool down.

"You play the fiddle?" Walter was always delighted to meet a fellow musician.

"I've been known to rosin the bow from time to time."

Walter lifted the fiddle up to him.

"Well, give her a try."

Reeves worked his way through a breakdown, and the violin sounded as good close under his ear as it had from across the room, which wasn't always the case.

"What do you call that tune?" Walter asked.

"Over the Road to Maysville."

"That's a Kentucky tune, ain't it?"

"I grew up in Barthell, Kentucky, in a coal camp."

"Play one more. I like what you can do with a fiddle."

So Reeves launched into his version of *Lost Indian*, and played it through twice while other members of the band nodded and smiled. Then he handed the fiddle back to Walter.

"That is a mighty fine instrument," Reeves said. "You know a man would pay a good price for a violin like that."

Walter smiled. "No amount of money can separate me

from this fiddle, mister. It was a gift from my dear departed wife. She raised eggs for a year to pay for it."

"Eggs?" Reeves asked, but Walter just laughed, which made the foreman chafe.

"But I'm talking about real, cash money. Look, these are hard times, and everyone can use a little money."

"I could use more than a little," Walter said with a chuckle, thinking about how he made from the store and post office. The trouble was, he found it difficult to say no to people. They would feed him a hard luck story and ask for credit, just for a month or two, you know, until they could get back on their feet again, or until the baby came, or their son sent them money from Omaha where he found work in the stockyards. Walter would write the amounts down next to their names in his book and let them carry the food, shoes, and seed corn out of his store knowing he would likely never see a penny for it. But what else could he do? They were his neighbors, his friends. If only the Big Money men would let Mr. Roosevelt turn things around, that is what he prayed for.

Reeves waited a couple of days before visiting the store to work on Walter some more. His lust for the violin had taken possession of him, and he wasn't the kind of person to let anyone or anything stand in the way of what he wanted.

"Here's two-hundred-and-forty dollars, cash," Reeves said, peeling off two-dozen ten-dollar bills and laying them on the counter, one after the other, for effect.

Walter wheeled his chair up close, gazed at the money, and sighed.

"Don't reckon I've seen that many sawbucks in one stack for I don't know how long. But look here, Reeves," he spun the chair around to face the foreman. "I'm not in the market to sell. There are plenty of good violins in the world; I'll just keep the one I have."

It came to Reeves then that the old man would not be moved by money or any other enticement. The foreman would have to come up with an alternative plan.

Several days later Reeves was shooting eight-ball at Skinner's pool hall with a crowd of the town loafers when he struck up a conversation with a young man named Eddie Townsend, Walter Hendricks' nephew. As a foreman who hired and fired men as a matter of course, Reeves had become a pretty good judge of character over the years. He took in the young man's slothful manner, the way his eyes darted with worry to the door whenever it opened, like he owed money, and the way, after a couple of beers, (which Reeves gladly paid for) Ed bragged how he wasn't afraid of the law or anybody else.

Yep, Reeves thought to himself, he's just the fellow I'm looking for. And he saw no reason to waste time going all the way around the barn to get to the point.

"Look here, Eddie. You seem like a bright young fellow and I'm going to be square with you. Your uncle has a violin that I'd give my eyeteeth to own. You know the one I'm talking about?"

Ed nodded his head. "It's got as pretty a maple back as you could hope to find. It's like the fiddle's on fire."

"Yep, that's the very one. I offered to buy the violin. Hell, I offered your uncle twice what it's worth, but he turned me down. It left me discouraged, to tell you the truth."

"Uncle Walter can be a stubborn son-of-a-gun once his mind is set. Just how high are you willing to go to get that violin?"

Reeves knew in then that, even though Eddie was a layabout, he had a nose for opportunity.

"I'd go as high as three hundred dollars."

Eddie scratched his chin and whistled.

"That sure ain't pocket change, mister!"

"A man could live for a year on that much money without doing a lick of work," the foreman pressed his opening. "Of course, I don't much care who gets the money so long as I get the fiddle. We're about done with the pipeline and just in time, what with the weather turning cold, and snow on the way. I'll be leaving this town soon and don't reckon I'll ever be back. Sure hate to leave without that violin and the money still in my pocket. Well," he shrugged, "I guess some things can't be helped. Let me buy you another beer and we'll shoot a game of pool."

They racked up the balls and Reeves didn't mention the fiddle again.

The next afternoon when the foreman came into the pool hall, Eddie was ready for him. "You still wanting that fiddle?" he asked the older man, his voice lowered so as not to be overheard.

"I'll tell a man I do," said Reeves.

"And you ain't too particular about how it comes your way?"

"That's not really my concern, is it? I'll give the money to any man who turns it over to me."

"Is the price still three hundred dollars?"

Reeves nodded.

"Let's take a little walk. I have an idea I want to talk over with you."

They walked down Hickory Street, past the feed store and the shoe repair shop until they reached the old bridge that crossed the river to the railroad switching yard. But it wasn't until they started up the tracks that Eddie laid out his plan.

"My uncle always goes to church of a Wednesday evening. Someone comes by the house and fetches him around six o'clock and takes him over and brings him back. So I'm thinking as tomorrow is Wednesday, maybe I'll hide myself in the woods across the road from his place and, after he's gone to church, I'll slip in and snatch the fiddle."

Everything was going along as Reeves predicted it would with a man like Eddie. And yet he had to ask, "Don't it bother you none, stealing from your own kin?"

Eddie stopped walking and looked at Reeves, the soles of his shoes grinding the cinders by the track as he turned and faced the bigger man. "I don't know as if I'd call it stealing. Ever since my aunt died, Uncle Walter ain't been the same. I doubt he'll last out the winter. My mother says it's like that when a husband and wife are very close. One dies, and pretty soon, before you know it, the other goes, too. And what will happen to the fiddle then? It'll just get auctioned off for a few bucks with the rest of his belongings. That'd be an awful waste, as I see it."

"From what I understand," Reeves put in, "your uncle never had any children. Maybe he left the fiddle to you in his will. Maybe he left you his house and everything else."

Eddie sneered. "Me and my uncle ain't that close. We used to be, but we ain't no more."

Reeves considered asking what caused the falling out, but he didn't really care. He was just glad young Eddie wasn't about to scruple the theft and sale of his uncle's violin.

"Do you have a way to get over to your uncle's house tomorrow evening?"

"I figured on walking," said Eddie.

"No, I'll drive you over in my truck. Is there someplace we can park on the other side of the woods?"

"Yeah, sure. The woods come out on another road."

"Good, then that's what we'll do. I'll have the money with me."

"Pick me up in back of the pool hall at five o'clock," Eddie said, showing some animation. "It'll be near dark by then, so nobody will see us go off together."

That night brought the first snowfall of the winter, about four inches. By morning the sky had cleared, and Reeves wound up the pipeline project, paid off the crew, and saw to the loading of the equipment. Just before five o'clock, he drove into town and turned into the alley that ran behind the pool hall. Eddie was standing outside in the cold, smoking a cigarette. He got into the truck, blowing on his hands to warm them up.

"Head north out of town. It's about three miles. You got the money with you?"

"Don't worry about the money," Reeves said, patting his stomach where he wore his money belt. "It's right here."

Eddie pulled a short, flat bottle from his coat pocket. He unscrewed the cap and took a pull on it. The smell of cheap whiskey filled the cab of the truck. He held the bottle out to Reeves, but the foreman shook his head.

"Suit yourself," Eddie said and took another swallow before stuffing the bottle back into his pocket.

They drove on in silence for several miles, until Eddie spoke again.

"Turn left here. This road'll bring us around the far side of the woods."

"You're going to go through with this, right? And then keep mum?" Reeves was gauging the risk. Eddie was far from being his choice partner in crime.

"Of course I am. I ain't no coward."

"I wasn't saying you were. Just wanted to be sure."

"When are you leaving town?"

"Tomorrow sometime. I'll winter in Alabama. The company's got us scheduled to go to Illinois in the spring."

"Good. If the sheriff starts nosing around looking for that fiddle, I want it long gone."

Half a mile farther on, they began to skirt a wood that ran along the right side of the road. At Eddie's instruction, Reeves turned onto an abandoned logging road and drove a short way into the trees before stopping. Reeves cut the engine and Eddie jumped out.

"This shouldn't take long. I'll get the fiddle as soon as my uncle leaves for church."

"Did you bring a flashlight?"

"Don't need one. The moon's already up, and with all this snow, I can see my way just fine."

It was less than a third of a mile through the woods to the road that ran in front of Hendricks' Store. Eddie sheltered just inside the tree line. He took occasional sips of whiskey and watched the smoke drift from his uncle's chimney into the frosty night air. There were half a dozen houses stretched up and down the road, but he saw no one moving about. Then he heard the sound of a truck coming down the road. It pulled up in front of the store with the engine running and the lights on. Two men got out and went in the front door, and a minute later they carried out his Uncle Walter. They lifted their passenger into the cab of the truck, tied the wheelchair to the flatbed, and drove off.

Eddie wasted no time. As soon as the sound of the truck faded away, he slipped out of the woods and crossed the road in the moonlight. He snuck around the building to the back porch, half of which served as a wood shed. Instead of stairs leading from the ground to the porch, there was a wooden ramp with a sturdy handrail. Eddie climbed the ramp. The back door had a glass window, and even though Eddie knew there was a key on the ledge above the door, he wanted it to look like a burglary. The neighboring homes were far enough away that he didn't fear being heard. He picked up a chunk of wood and busted the window. He reached through, unlocked the door, and stepped into the kitchen. His uncle lived in several rooms separated from the store and post office, and Eddie pictured the layout in his mind. The kitchen led directly into a sitting room. To the right of the sitting room was a short hallway, wide enough for Walter's wheelchair, with a bedroom on one side and an office with a roll top desk on the other side. At the end of the hallway was a bathroom fitted with cast iron pipes screwed to the walls so his uncle could use the toilet and lift himself in and out of the bathtub.

Eddie paused a moment and listened. The only sound was the lazy crackle of the woodstove. He recalled that the old man kept the violin on a small round table in the sitting room, so he headed that way. Walter's sitting room was illuminated by the moonlight that streamed in through the side window. On the wall near the woodstove was a large, oval, gilt-edged picture frame. Inside the frame was a photograph of his late aunt. The sight of his aunt filled the young intruder with a rush of memories. Whereas his uncle could be hard and unforgiving as flint, Aunt Emma was always warm and welcoming. She would give him something to eat whenever he came to visit and ask him questions. What are you up to these days, Eddie? How do you like school? Do you have a girlfriend yet?

No one else ever asked him about his life, not his parents, who had too many kids and too little money to pay much attention. Nor did Uncle Walter or any of the other relatives for that matter. But Aunt Emma made him feel as if she was genuinely interested, and Eddie suddenly missed her kindly ways.

Now, with Emma peering down at him from the oval picture frame, Eddie felt small and mean. He sensed her presence in the house as if she were still alive and might walk in from the kitchen at any moment. He even imagined he detected the scent of her perfume. And he knew she was disappointed in him. The shame burned his cheeks. Suddenly he decided he couldn't go through with it. He couldn't violate the trust she had placed in him. He might have already thrown his soul away, but he'd be hanged if he'd sink to betraying his own flesh and blood. Turning on his heel, he hurried from of the house, leaving the fiddle untouched in its case on the small round table.

When he got back to the truck, he was cold and irritable.

"Let's get out of here," he said, slamming the door.

"Where's the fiddle?" Reeves asked without touching the starter button.

"There ain't going to be no goddamn fiddle."

"What do mean? Didn't your uncle go to church?"

"Yeah, he went to church."

"And was his fiddle in the house?"

"Yeah, it was in the sitting room, like always."

"Then why didn't you bring it back with you? You want the money, don't you?" Eddie's sulky manner was getting on

Reeves' nerves, and he could feel his anger rising.

"You can keep your money. I ain't going to rob the old man. It ain't right."

"Well, this is a fine time to get religion," Reeves snorted. "You dragged me all the way out here and made me sit in a cold truck for the better part of an hour expecting to get that fiddle and, by God, I aim to have it. Now you go back and fetch it!"

Eddie made no move to get out of the truck but dug around in his coat pocket for his bottle.

"I said get moving, you worthless rounder. I'll not be trifled with!"

Startled by the anger and menace in the older man's voice, Eddie swung open the truck door and climbed out. "Hell, I'll just walk back to town."

Reeves was seething. He was tempted to jump out of the truck and beat the crap out of Eddie, teach him a lesson. Of all the stupid stunts he had ever been a party to. Instead, he just sat behind the steering wheel and watched Eddie walk down the logging road, the young man's elbow lifting as he took another swig from his bottle.

After a couple of minutes, Reeves reached under the truck seat and withdrew a thirty-two caliber, nickel-plated revolver, which he dropped into his coat pocket. Grumbling to himself, "If you want something done right, you've got to do it yourself," he set off through the woods in the direction of the store, following Eddie's footsteps in the snow.

He crossed the road and continued following the tracks around the back of the house to the porch. After climbing the ramp, he inspected the broken window before trying the doorknob. Eddie had not reset the lock.

He stepped inside and passed through the kitchen into

the moonlit sitting room. The fiddle case was on the table, and he went over to it. Grabbing it by the handle, he turned to confront the image of a woman in an oval picture frame staring down at him. For a moment he was powerless to move his legs as a sickening wave of reproach and fear surged through him. It was a familiar feeling, one he experienced often as a boy just before his father beat him with the razor strop for some transgression or other. He felt the eyes in the portrait boring into his own. A light seemed to shimmer about the oval frame. His palms started to clam and sweat. This was no mere photograph, he sensed, but a living soul. A log burning in the stove slid down against the cast iron side, making a clang. Reeves struggled to calm his erratic breathing. He had a choice to make: set down the violin and flee the house, or master the irrational terror that threatened to unman him.

"I fear you not, old woman," he croaked, "be you ghost or devil. And I'm taking this violin for my own and you be damned!"

Reeves willed his legs to move and he made for the back door. He slipped going down the icy ramp, but managed to regain his balance. Clutching the violin, he hurried across the road and entered the dark woods. All was still and quiet except for the crunch of his boots on the snow. He struggled to gain control of his emotions, and it took some time before he realized that he had lost the track of his footprints in the snow. He assumed he was walking in the general direction of the truck, but wasn't exactly sure where he was.

"Stop worrying," he scolded himself, his breath clouding up in the frigid night air. "You'll find the road easy enough when you reach the other side of these woods."

The moon shone down through the branches of the bare

trees, casting long shadows across his snowy path.

Crunch, crunch, crunch—step after step. The air was breathless, the woods stark and empty.

Then through the cold silence he thought he heard something. He stopped and listened. Faintly, from what seemed a great distance, he heard music. Perhaps someone in one of the houses near the store was playing the Victrola or the radio. He took a few more steps and stopped again. The music sounded closer. He looked among the trunks of the trees but saw nothing. He trained his ears on the sound. It was a fiddle. He rubbed his dry lips with his free hand. No, it wasn't a fiddle. It was someone singing a fiddle tune, and it was coming closer. He was in a blue panic now, and his mind went back in time to when he and his mother would visit his grandmother at the state mental asylum in Weston. It was a terrifying place. He recalled one woman in particular. Dressed in a soiled nightgown, all she did was walk in circles and sing to herself, her hair matted and filthy.

"Why is she singing, Mama?" he asked.

"Her mind's wandering," was all his mother would say.

Reeves started off again, picking up his pace so that the crunching of his boots drowned out the singing for a while. But then he heard it again, louder and closer, as if someone were stalking him.

Terror gripped him, and he started to run, kicking up snow with each step. Several times he stumbled and dropped to his knees, cursing, looking back over his shoulder, straining to catch sight of his pursuer. His breath came in sharp, painful stabs. The woods were endless. The singer was close, very close, just behind him.

Reeves halted, panting and exhausted. The knees of his

trousers were soaked and the cold and exertion made his lungs hurt. A sudden desperate anger blazed up in him and he swung around to confront his tormentor. To free his right hand, he dropped the fiddle case, the thump muffled by the snow. He drew his revolver from his pocket.

Six pistol shots exploded and echoed through the dark empty woods, startling the night creatures, only for the echoes to be swallowed up again by the winter stillness.

The next morning was crisp and bright, and Glenn Martin, a local trapper, came upon a dead man in the snow. He went and fetched the sheriff. The deceased was identified as one James Arthur Reeves, foreman for a construction company that had just completed a pipeline through the county. Reeves was found lying on his back with an empty revolver clutched in his right hand.

During the autopsy, the coroner found no indication of an external wound; neither did he find evidence of heart attack or stroke. In the end, he filled in the certificate with the words, "Death from exposure."

There was another part to this strange occurrence that baffled the authorities. In the snow next to the dead man, the sheriff found the distinct imprint of a fiddle case, but no instrument was recovered from the scene. There were two sets of footprints, those of the dead man and the trapper who found him, but no sign of anyone else ever having been there. So what had happened to the fiddle case? Glenn Martin was known to be an honest man, and he swore he never touched it. He swore he never even saw it. And no one else could explain what happened.

Walter Hendricks returned from church that evening to find the window of his back door broken, pieces of glass scattered on the kitchen floor. He suspected a robbery, but after a thorough search he found nothing missing. He went to bed planning to call the sheriff in the morning.

Early the next day, however, everyone was talking about the dead man found in the woods, and Walter wondered if he had anything to do with his broken window.

He made one more search and discovered something unusual. The doily that covered the round table in the sitting room where he kept his fiddle was damp. He couldn't understand why. The bottom of the fiddle case felt damp as well.

He looked up at Emma's portrait.

"Do you know what's going on here?" he asked.

There was no reply. Walter shrugged and put the mystery out of his mind.

Later that evening, as was his custom before turning in, he opened the case and took out his fiddle. He wheeled his chair around so he could look at Emma's portrait as he played her favorite tune. It was a waltz titled *Forget-Me-Not*.

GOING
DOWN
THE
RIVER

Buck Sullivan grew up along the banks of the Ohio River in a town called Parkersburg in what is now West Virginia, but back then was part of Virginia, the Old Dominion. His father, a native-born Irishman, ran a dry goods store with his wife who was full-blooded Shawnee.

Buck was the baby of the family. His two older brothers took after their father in appearance, having fair, freckled skin and light hair. Buck was like his mother with hair black as a crow's wing and eyes like pools of dark water.

He was different in other ways, too. Whereas his brothers were boisterous and full of mischief, fighting and drinking whenever they had the chance, Buck was of a quiet disposition. The one time he did indulge in alcoholic spirits, when he was sixteen, he got dreadfully sick and his head hurt for days.

"Why am I so different from my brothers?" Buck asked his mother one day when he was seven and they were alone together in the store.

"Come, sit next to me," she said, and she took his hands in her own and looked at him a long moment before speaking.

"You are my son and I love you very much. So does your father. But he is not your real father."

Buck didn't know what to make of this.

"Is another man my father?"

"No, not a man."

"I don't understand."

His mother's features were a mixture of happiness and sorrow.

"One night before you were born I was restless and couldn't sleep. The walls of the house crowded in around me and I had trouble breathing. So I went outside for a walk. I was alone and the moon was full and I walked until I came to the river. The bright silver moonlight danced upon the surface of the water and I heard the river singing. Its song was so beautiful and restful that I grew drowsy and I lay down on the grass of the riverbank and fell asleep. I had a dream, a very powerful dream."

She paused but continued to hold Buck's hands.

"What was the dream, Mother?"

"I dreamt the spirit of the river came and caressed me, filling my belly with a child. When I awoke, it was early morning. I hurried home, but I told no one about my dream. Nine months later you were born and I knew that your father was the river. He is a mighty father, my son, and he will look after you. You are lucky to have such a father."

Buck didn't know what to believe. His mother often talked about mountains, the wind, animals, even waterfalls, in the same way she talked about a customer or neighbor. To her these elements and creatures of the natural world had souls and personalities, the same as people. Was it possible for the river to be his father? He wanted to ask his teacher or brothers but feared they would laugh at him, which would be laughing at his mother, too. Yet he never forgot what she told him.

The years passed, and Buck found himself drawn to the spirited music of the fiddle. Some of the men who crewed the flatboats and keelboats that plied the river played the fiddle and Buck would go down to the levee after dark to hear them play. He also enjoyed their rambunctious tall tales and funny songs.

Oh, my little girl, if you don't do better,
Put you on the boat, gonna send you down the river;
Boat began to sink, my heart began to quiver,
Oh, my little girl, you're going down the river.

One evening, a red-haired fiddler beckoned him to board his flatboat. "You seem partial to the sound of the fiddle, young man," he said good-naturedly. "Ever tucked one up under your chin?"

Buck, who was now thirteen, shook his head.

"Here then, have a go with mine. Don't be skittish; it won't bite."

Two deck hands perched atop the cargo hold grinned at Buck in a way that caused the young man's cheeks to burn with embarrassment.

"Don't pay them no never mind," the red-haired man laughed. "With this sorry lot, the sourer the music, the more they like it."

So Buck drew the bow across the strings and from that moment he was hooked as surely as the five-foot-long sturgeon he once caught while fishing with his brothers. He was going to learn how to play the fiddle come what may.

"What will it cost me for a good fiddle?"

"You can get a decent one for two dollars."

"I've got that much saved up," Buck bragged.

The red-haired fiddler smiled and yelled to his friends, "The youngster says he's got money." The other men nodded and grinned some more.

"I'll tell you what, young fella," the riverman said. "We leave first thing in the morning. We're going down to Cairo and I know a man there who deals in violins. You bring me your money and on the return trip I'll bring you a violin."

"But I don't want a violin," Buck said. "I want a fiddle."

Again the man laughed. "Son, a violin and fiddle are the same instrument. It just comes down to what kind of music you play on 'em. So what do you say? Shall I bring you a violin?"

Buck was at the dock before sunup and he gave the boatman his two dollars, which was all the money he had in the world. He earned it unloading boats when there weren't enough men available to do the work.

"It'll be two months before we pass this way going north," the boatman told him. "How can I get word to you?"

Buck told him about the dry goods store and where to find it.

"Good. I'll see you then."

Buck watched the men pole their flatboat away from the bank in the grey morning light until the current took hold and carried it down the river, the red-haired fiddler manning one of the sweep oars and waving.

Buck could hardly think straight for the next two months as he waited for his violin. He asked around to see if anyone could teach him how to play the fiddle, and was directed to a farmer north of town named Abel Justice. Several people said Farmer Justice was the best fiddler in the area, so Buck went and talked to him.

"There's a good chance you'll never see a fiddle or your two dollars again," Abel Justice told him. "Rivermen aren't to be trusted."

"But he is a fiddler and a good one, too."

"That don't signify. Rivermen are a breed apart, or they used to be. Nowadays you find all kinds: farmers, shopkeepers, retired soldiers—even women, and lots of 'em have loved ones at home waiting for 'em to return. Now you take the farmer living near the river. He will cobble a boat together with boards he's milled from trees cut on his own land and then he'll load it with his harvest and float it all the way down to New Orleans where he hopes he'll get a good price. Maybe his sons will come along to help steer the boat or he'll hire a couple of men. I've even heard of a preacher piloting a flatboat down the river so he could earn enough money to build a new church."

"What do they do with the boats once they get there?"

"Bust 'em up and sell 'em for firewood."

"Then how do they get home?"

"They pay for passage on a steamboat. Back when I was a sapling, before the steamboats come along, men who made the trip had to ride shank's mare to get home and that took months. That's why there were fewer boatmen back then. They liked to brag and call themselves "alligator horses," claiming they were half alligator and half horse. And I'll tell you this: you took care not to cross one for fear he'd draw his knife and gut you like a pike and leave you to rot. Why I've heard of companies of flatboatmen taking over a whole town and doing with it whatever came into their heads. No, it's better now, thanks to the steamboats, even though they make a racket and fill the air with fulsome smoke."

Despite Abel Justin's suspicions, however, the red-haired fiddler proved true to his word. Buck was in the back of the store sweeping out the storeroom when the boatman walked in carrying a violin case. Buck's mother was working the counter and she called for Buck to come up front. When the boatman handed Buck the case, Buck cradled it as if it were newborn.

"Well, don't you want to open it and see what kind of violin I brung you?" the man said.

Buck laid the case on the counter and opened it. The violin, dark brown with a black ebony fingerboard and tailpiece, was the prettiest thing he had ever seen.

"It has known some use," the riverman said, "but that only makes a violin sound better, in my opinion. Best of all, it notes true and you can learn on it,"

Buck was little help around the store for some time after that; he was constantly slipping away to saw on his fiddle. Farmer Justice showed him how to hold the instrument so that his arm didn't get sore and how to tune it depending on the melody he wanted to play.

"And make sure to keep the fiddle away from mice," he told Buck one day.

"Why is that?" Buck asked.

"Because it makes a cozy home for a mother mouse to have her young in. Darned near ruined a fiddle I owned some years ago. The mouse gnawed a big hole right in the middle of the f hole."

"Did it ruin the sound?"

"No, it just looked bad. So I told people the fiddle had stopped an Indian arrow and saved my life."

"But I thought you said a mouse made the hole?"

The farmer laughed. "Well, you see, folks expect fiddlers to stretch the blanket now and again, adds a dash of zip and wonder to their humdrum lives. So if you're going to play the fiddle, make sure to store up some good yarns to go along with the tunes you play. That way you'll be welcome wherever you go."

When it came to trapping a tune and taming it, Buck relied on his ears and the rhythms of his heart. Playing the fiddle was like something he had done before; the music came that naturally to him.

Soon Buck was entertaining the store's customers with his fiddle playing. They loved his music and told their friends and the friends came to the store and that helped business.

Then during the summer when Buck was sixteen, he traveled east to the settlement of Clarksburg to compete in his first fiddle contest. It was an arduous journey because the roads weren't much to speak of back then. All the same, it was worth the trip because Buck won the contest and they gave him three shiny silver dollars for his prize. He was so proud of having won the money that, as soon as he got home, he drilled two small holes in the center of each coin. He then asked his mother to stitch the coins along the backside of his leather belt. He boasted that he had the fanciest belt in six counties.

When Buck was seventeen, his father's heart gave out, and his oldest brother, Frank, took over the store. Frank wanted to open another store in a nearby town and asked Buck to run it.

"Folks will flock to the store to hear that fiddle of yours. And after four or five years you'll be able to buy me out and the store will be yours: lock, stock, and barrel."

It was a generous offer, and Buck knew he should jump at the chance, but a restlessness had entered his soul, a yearning for something he couldn't quite name.

"It will soon be time for you to take a wife," his mother told him. "Maybe that is why you are unhappy."

"But I want to see some of the world first before I get married," Buck said.

"If I were you," said Clyde, the middle brother, "I'd go east across the mountains. They have a bunch of big cities back east and you're bound to find work. There's Philadelphia and New York and the capitol where the president lives."

Buck thought about this for several days and was of half a mind to follow Clyde's advice when he had a dream. In the dream he was floating down the river at night. The river stretched out wide and dark on both sides of him, and he hummed a soft melody as he stared up into an obsidian sky shot through with twinkling stars. He felt a depth of peace unlike any he had known before, and when he awoke he went and told his mother about his dream.

"Your father sent the dream to you," she said.

"But what does it mean?" Buck asked, although in his heart he already knew.

"You should follow the river. It will take you many places and you will find what you need."

So Buck began to make preparations to leave home and follow the river. He said goodbye to old friends including his fiddle teacher, Abel Justice.

"Be careful of the company you keep," the old man advised him. "It's not always easy to read character. You're young and tend to see the best in people. But that can lead you into trouble. I know, I was young once myself, although you wouldn't know it now to look at me."

"Did you get in trouble?" Buck asked.

"I played the fool, I'm not too proud to admit it. But the One above watched over me. Remember what He told us: "Behold, I send you forth as sheep in the midst of wolves: be ye therefore wise as serpents, and harmless as doves.""

Buck had never heard Farmer Justice quote scripture. He didn't think the old man was even religious. Buck's father used to take him and his brothers to church, but it always felt strange because his mother stayed at home.

"And one more thing," Abel Justice continued, "avoid talking politics with people you don't know. There's trouble coming, just mark my words."

"What kind of trouble?"

"Slavery is going to tear this nation apart. We got it stuck in our craw; we can't swallow it and can't spit it out. Then, too, there's the Indian problem. You're part injun. It ain't right how we've treated them folks. I mean it was their land and we just come along and took it. Sent 'em packing, those we didn't kill with our diseases. Sent 'em way the heck out west. But we'll be wanting that land, too, before long. You can bet on it. And where are the Indians going to go to then?"

Buck knew better than to interrupt the old man when he was on a tear. The farmer would bob his head up and down and smack the table so hard with the palm on his hand the pewter cups and plates would rattle.

Buck was fond of the farmer and appreciated everything he had taught him about the fiddle and about life and its injustices. Funny how someone can have a name that fits him so well.

When it came to being part Shawnee, Buck did his best to ignore the fact. It came up from time to time, had to, given his looks. A student at school would call him a name and he would have to fight the boy. But he didn't feel like an Indian. Maybe that was because he never met his mother's family. They had all gone west before he was born. Even the business about being the son of the river grated on him sometimes. That was Indian talk and he was an American and being an American was plenty good enough for him.

On the day before he left home, Buck's mother gave him a box containing a matched pair of dueling pistols. The decoratively carved black walnut stocks and the scroll engraving on the lock plates and the rear of each barrel were the work of a skilled gunsmith. Also in the box were a powder flask, cleaning rods, and a bullet mold.

"Take these with you," his mother told him, "they will protect you."

Buck was surprised by the gift. He had no desire to carry a weapon. He was a musician, not a fighter. But he did not wish to hurt his mother's feelings.

"How did you come to own these?" he asked her.

"A man owed us a large sum of money which he could not pay, so he gave us these instead. They belonged to his grandfather who was a colonel during the war in 1812."

"But they must be very valuable."

"May they keep you safe."

The next morning, Buck said an emotional farewell to his family and went down to the levee. With one hand he carried a carpetbag with the dueling pistol case strapped to the side and with the other he carried his fiddle case. Hanging from a cord around his neck and hidden beneath his shirt was a leather pouch containing the twenty gold coins his mother gave him. He was of two minds as to what to do: either use some of the money to pay for passage on a steamboat or see if he could find work on a steamboat and save the money for when he really needed it. When he reached the levee he found a half-dozen steamers, but they were all heading upriver toward Pittsburgh.

"A New Orleans bound packet should be along soon," a roustabout told him. The man was sitting on a drift log mending a mooring line.

"Can I get a job as a deck hand on your boat?" Buck asked.

"So you want to be a rooster? Ever worked on a steamboat?"

"No, but I've helped load cargo."

"It's different being a full-time deck hand. It's a rough life and no mistake."

"How is it a rough life?" Buck asked.

"Well, to start with they don't give deck hands a set place to sleep; you have to find some cramped space in among the cargo to throw down your blanket. And the food comes from the leavings of the passengers. The cook throws it all in a bucket and you have to reach in you paw along with all the other roosters to fish out enough to eat. Takes some getting used to."

"But I need to leave this town. I want to see the world."

"So you want to see the elephant?"

Buck was confused and it showed. The deck hand laughed. "I'm not talking about a real elephant, son. It's just a saying for something you don't see everyday."

"If you mean I aim to have me an adventure, then you're right as rain."

"Well, you'll find plenty adventures working on a steamboat, most of 'em bad. Hauling line for hours to drag the boat off a sandbar or clearing the wheel of tree branches and dead animals. But it's the bully boys you've got to look out for."

"What's a bully boy?" Buck asked.

"You are green," the roustabout laughed. "Bully boys are the mates on a steamboat and it's their job to keep us roosters in line. And since we carry knives, they carry guns and they don't hesitate to use 'em. Why, one time on board the *Spirit of Dixie*, I seen a mate shoot an Irishman in the head and dump him into the river."

"Why'd he do that?"

"Because the Irishman had a snoot full and thought he was Mike Fink. But it ain't right to plug a man and drop him in the river just 'cause nobody gives a straw for what happens to an Irishman. Maybe that fellow had a mother and father back home in Ireland and they never knew what happened to their boy. So that settled me, my oath it did, and the very next town we stopped at, I ran away from that boat. I wouldn't give that mate an excuse to shoot me."

Buck wasn't sure what to do.

"If I were you," the deck hand said, "I'd go down to where the flatboats are tied up. Look for one of the commercial boats. They're often short-handed and might let you work off your passage."

So Buck thanked the man for his advice and sauntered down to where forty or more flatboats were moored one next to the other like cord wood at the start of winter.

The first boat he approached was captained by a man named Barlow. A head shorter than Buck, he had a chest like a black bear and thick arms to match. His boat was fifty feet long and ten feet wide, and he commanded a crew of four whose job it was to man the steering oars while he controlled the rudder. His cargo for this trip downriver included stacks of tanned cattle hides, two dozen kegs of Pennsylvania whiskey, four crates of 50-caliber rifle barrels and percussion locks, and iron strapping to shod wagon wheels—the barrels and strapping produced in the forges along the Monongahela River near Pittsburgh.

"How far are you going?" Buck asked the captain.

"Depends. We trade our way downriver, sell our metal in one town and maybe take on cured hams, next town we might trade for salt. If it all works out we arrive in New Orleans with a boat full of cargo that the people there want to buy. This will be my tenth trip, and Curley, my first mate, he's been with me for seven of 'em. Ain't that right, Curley?" he called out and a man with tight curly brown hair stuck his head out of the cargo hatch.

"You want something, boss?"

"This town boy wants to join our crew. Can we use an extra hand?"

"There's always work on a flatboat for a man willing to do the work and ain't no complainer."

"I'm no complainer."

"I'm glad to hear it," the captain said. "Can you play that fiddle?"

"I can."

"A couple of years ago one of my men could saw out tunes on a fiddle. His name was Zack something or other. But the fool got drunk and got cut up pretty good in a knife fight in a saloon in Louisville and we had to leave him there. He was pretty bad off."

"Did he live?"

"I never heard," said the captain.

Curley guffawed. "Maybe Zack never heard neither."

This made the captain smile, too. "What Curley means is that Zack had both his ears sliced off, so maybe he couldn't hear none too good after that."

The captain tore the corner off a plug of tobacco with his teeth and began to chew. "Well, if you're coming, stash you gear below because we're about to cast off."

Buck's heart leapt at the realization that he was at last on his way. Clambering on board he found space in between the stack of cowhides to store his carpetbag, pistol box, and fiddle. Curley then showed him how to handle one of the long sweep oars that reached out into the water on each side of the boat.

The day was sunny with only an occasional breeze to soften the heat, and the river was crowded with other flatboats, keelboats, and great puffing steamboats. Slim, quick skiffs, like small fish, darted out from the farms and villages along the shore to do a bit of trading with the larger vessels that came by. Buck was learning how to right the boat using the long sweep oar. In between he leaned on the oar and surveyed the wide expanse of water and thought about his mother's story. Was it possible the river was his father? He didn't think so, and yet he felt a connection to the river as it pushed them along with its quiet strength that he could not put into words. When Curley came to spell him on the oar, he got out his fiddle and played the cheeriest tunes he knew, the notes skipping across the smooth water like flat stones and raising lusty shouts of approval from the crews and passengers of other boats. He played *The Wild Goose Chase* and *Magpie* and *Sugar in the Gourd*.

In a short while, Captain Barlow joined him, a crewman named Len taking a turn at the rudder.

"You can make that box sing," Barlow said, and he offered Buck his plug of tobacco. The young man declined and was about to launch into another tune when the captain said, "Do you know a tune called *Ida Red*?

"I do," Buck said.

"Ida was my mother's name. She died when I was three. My pappy was mean as a wolverine in heat but he taught me well."

Buck thought this a strange thing to say. He laid into a spirited rendition of *Ida Red*, but it brought no smile to the captain's face.

As daylight faded, many of the flatboats and rafts pulled for the shore so they could tie up for the night. Captain Barlow decided to run the river by the light of the quarter moon. Curley built a fire in a sand box on the foredeck and the crew gathered around to take their evening meal.

"Captain," Len said, "you told us that if we worked extra hard we could claim one of them whiskey kegs for our own."

"The pail is hanging on its nail," Barlow said, "Take it down and fetch us all some."

Len jumped up with a grin and went below. He came back with a pail filled with liquor. He also brought a tin cup and he dipped the cup into the bucket and handed it to Barlow. The captain drank down the contents in one long swallow, his eyes tearing. Then Len refilled the cup and gave it to Curley. When he offered Buck a cupful, Buck turned it down.

"Makes me crazy and sick," Buck said.

"Suit yourself," Len shrugged and drained the cup himself. Soon all the men on the boat were roaring drunk, even the captain. They took turns manning the rudder, but

Buck didn't think they were up to the task. He was worried they would run into another boat or raft in the dark, or hit a snag.

After a while the captain sent Len below again to refill the pail with whiskey, and when the riverman returned he was carrying the box containing the dueling pistols.

"That box is mine," Buck said, but Len ignored him. Buck looked to the captain but Barlow was arm wrestling Curley and couldn't be bothered. Len brought the box nearer the fire and opened it. The pistols gleamed in the firelight.

"Look at what I found, captain," he said.

Barlow pushed Curley's arm down and laughed. Then he turned his attention to the pistols.

"What's a spud like you doing with these darlings?"

"They were a gift from my mother," Buck said. His anger was rising but with it came a stronger emotion: fear. He had judged Barlow as a man of a steady turn, but now he saw he was mistaken. The captain was at heart a scoundrel, the very sort Farmer Justice had warned him about. How could he have been so blind?

"They belonged to a colonel who fought the British," Buck said.

"My grandpappy's brother fought the British," Curley said. "He was murdered by Indians after the battle of Frenchtown."

"Are they loaded?" the captain asked, ignoring Curley.

"No. I saw no reason to load them."

"A gun without powder and lead is as useless as a three-legged horse," Len said.

Buck wanted riverman to close the box and put it back where he found it, but he was afraid to say so.

"You've got a leather thong around your neck," the

captain said with a drunken sneer. "My guess is you've got a pouch full of money skulking beneath your shirt."

One of the riverman took the tin cup and filled it with whiskey from the pail. While he tilted his head back and drank, some of the liquor soaking his beard, the other men stared at Buck.

"How much money is in that pouch of yours?" Curley asked.

"That's my business," Buck said.

"Everything on this boat is *my* business," the captain barked, "and don't you forget it."

"You can keep the pistols," Buck offered. "I make a gift of them to you."

"And what about the pouch and the money?" Barlow asked, his words beginning to slur.

"I need the money to live on until I find work," Buck said, and he noticed the captain give his mate a sidelong glance as if they both knew something he didn't.

"What I want is that belt he's wearing," Len said. "Where did you get such a pretty thing?"

"I won the coins in a fiddle contest," Buck replied.

"You play that box of yours right good," said Curley.

"It comes easy to me."

"Well, you might play like a white man," Len cut in, "but you've got the look of an Injun and I have no truck with Injuns.

The captain stood, swayed, and put his hand on the roof of the cargo hold to steady himself. He peered into the darkness to see if any boats were near by. Buck looked too, but he saw no lights.

"Son, I'm sorry to tell you this," Barlow said with a tone that could be confused with fatherly concern if the listener didn't know better. "But it's your misfortune to have fallen in among bad men. We want more than your pistols. We aim to take everything you own."

With a sinking feeling of dread, Buck watched as Barlow pulled a huge Bowie knife from out of a sheath that hung on his belt. The polished blade glittered in the firelight. "This be 'Pet.' That's his name. And he's a faithful pet, isn't he, boys?"

"He's only got one tooth but it's sharp enough," said Len.

The boatmen were all grinning now, like rabid foxes. An expectation of blood was in the air and that excited them. They licked their lips. Buck again cast his gaze about. They were in the middle of the river, half a mile or more to either shore. If he called out for help, no one would hear him.

"Strip off that belt of yours," the captain ordered and Buck obeyed.

"Now hand over the pouch."

Buck slipped the pouch from around his neck and handed that over, too. The captain tossed the coin-filled pouch in the air and caught it in the palm of his left hand, pleased with the heft of it. In his right hand he held the blade pointed at Buck's heart.

"Will you let me live?" Buck asked. "I've done you no harm."

"That's the trouble with robbery," the captain said. "It requires killing, too.

"But I don't want the things you've taken. Just leave me my fiddle, that's all I ask, and I will go my way with no bitter feelings."

"No," the captain shook his head, "we can't have you going to the authorities after the fear has worn off and you feel all safe and righteous inside."

"You wouldn't want to do this if you weren't drunk," Buck said, trying to keep his voice from breaking.

The captain laughed. "Son, men get drunk so they have the nerve to do what they really want to do. Ain't that right, boys?"

The other men nodded, except for Curley whose expression was more confused than criminal.

"He's younger than my kid brother, boss," Curley whined.

"If you don't have the stomach for this business, Curley, you can go down below."

Curley looked at the faces of his crewmates and saw their determination.

"No, I'll stay," he said.

"Good. Then it's best we end this here and now," Barlow said, the knife poised to strike. "If you have any praying to do, lad, now's the time to do it."

Len took swig of whiskey, his eyes red and watery. Buck had never felt so utterly alone and defenseless.

"The only prayers I know are my tunes. Allow me to play my fiddle just once more to say goodbye to life."

The captain looked at the other crewmembers. The lust for murder was upon them, but they could wait. He nodded his head.

Buck opened his fiddle case and took out the instrument. He stood and put the violin to his chin and began to play. But it wasn't a cheery tune like the ones he had played before, no reel or hornpipe. Instead, it was the kind of tune he sometimes played late at night after everyone had gone to bed, a tune that made itself up as it went along, slow and mournful to stir up old memories and coax obscure, unsatisfied feelings from their hiding places deep within the heart. Longings. Regrets. The need to forgive and be forgiven. Then the notes changed their course and flowed into a melody about the river back when he was child. Nights spent fishing with his brothers on the muddy bank, his pole with the bark skinned off, reaching out over the water reflecting the flickering light of the campfire, the surrounding blackness sprinkled with fireflies and the hooting of an owl. Then the tune went back in time even further, back to the days before the white people came crowding into the valley, conjuring up images of a ghost-like mist lying low on the water in the early morning as brightly colored leaves, newly fallen, float by. There, too, among the notes was the beating of wings as a flock of geese set off for their day's journey south, and the sudden splash of a fat bass feeding on a dragonfly. His music shifted again and an image arose of a mighty river held prisoner by winter ice, the wind herding the snow across the still surface, a landscape of loneliness and waiting. Now he was playing for his father. He no longer doubted his mother's story. He knew the truth in the very marrow of his bones. The river was the force that flowed through his music, always had, just as his blood flowed through the veins of his body, pulsing with an ancient beat as old as time itself. He thanked his father with all of his heart for the precious gifts of life and music.

The music ceased. In the silence, the gentle lapping of the water against the hull of the flatboat made its own kind of music, bewitching and solemn. The boatmen, stupefied by what they had just heard, could only watch as Buck stooped to place the fiddle back inside its case. He then straightened up, gripped the captain's eyes with his own for the span of several heartbeats, before leaping onto the gunwale of the boat and diving into the river.

The splash was a cannon shot, causing the startled men to jump to their feet. They peered into the blackness but could see or hear nothing. Curley ran and returned with an oil-soaked torch. He plunged its head into the flames of the fire and then held it aloft over the edge of the boat in hopes of glimpsing the boy. But Buck was gone.

"He'll not go far," Barlow said with a certainty born of years of experience working the river. "The current will take him soon enough. Forget about him." He turned his attention to their ill-gotten treasures.

Buck too accepted the futility of trying to swim to the shore against the powerful current. He would exhaust himself long before reaching the safety of dry land. Nor was he afraid of dying; he just wanted to choose the manner of his death. Much better to sink into the arms of his father, he thought, than be butchered like a beef for market. He swam away from the boat until he was sure they would not pursue him. He then let himself slip beneath the surface, giving himself to the river. Deeper and deeper he sank, his lighter arms and legs trailing above him as he waited for the moment when he could no longer hold his breath and would fill them with water and death. He felt no panic. Instead, the same peace he had experienced in his dream stole over him. Closing his eyes, he felt the pressure push against his eardrums as he sank deeper.

Then something like a giant hand came up from below and lifted him gently toward the surface. Only it wasn't a hand with five fingers. It was a hand with hundreds of fingers, a thousand fingers, all quivering and darting as one, their combined mass making for him a sort of living raft. His head broke the surface of the water and he beheld stars overhead, brilliant and welcoming. He filled his grateful lungs with the cool night air. All about him was shimmering silver and he realized he was being held afloat by an immense school of fish. Where had they come from? He didn't need to ask. His father had heard him play and sent his creatures to save him.

The fish moved him through the water at a dizzying speed. In the distance he saw a low, dark shape approaching. It was an island, long and thin, that stood out some distance from the river's western shore. The fish carried him to within a hundred feet of the head of the island, where the swift current split in two and ran down either side. There the fish dropped away into the depths, and he had to use all his strength to swim the last narrow expanse of water to safety.

With the current still tugging at him, he managed to grab the thick, slime-clad root of a tree and pull himself up onto land. He lay upon his back exhausted but his exhilaration knew no bounds. He laughed and cried. He thanked his father. Then, glistening wet from his watery passage, he drifted off into dreamless, comforting sleep.

The bawl of a steamboat whistle called Buck back from the land of nod. It was early morning, and already the river was alive with traffic. The lowing of cattle came to him from across the water where a large raft crowded with livestock floated low in the water down the center channel of the river. It was this obstruction that gave the impatient steamboat cause to complain. Buck could hear angry men's voices shouting back and forth across the water, and he thought back to his rescue of the previous night. Again he thanked his father, then set off to explore the island.

Halfway down the island he came upon a camp. All about the camp were huge stacks of cordwood. A makeshift cabin sat back against a copse of trees, smoke pouring from a squat chimney made of sticks and dry mud. At the water's edge stood a landing with a half dozen pilings sticking up out of the water for boats to tie up to. South of the camp for some distance the island was denuded of trees.

As Buck approached the cabin a black dog charged him from out of the open door. The dog came to within a few feet, then stopped and began to growl, baring its teeth. Buck cast about for a stick or rock with which to defend himself, when a man, balding and with short, bandy legs, issued from the cabin. He was armed with a shotgun pointed at the ground but in the direction of this unexpected visitor.

"Hello!" Buck shouted so he could be heard over the dog's growling. "I am stranded on your island." He didn't know if the man owned the island, he could be a squatter, but Buck felt it prudent to assume as much.

"Jack! Heel!" The man commanded and the dog ceased his growling, hid his teeth, and sank back on his haunches.

"A man needs a good dog if he hankers to live by himself," the man said with a smile. "My name is Menklin. Come inside, son, and tell me your story." Shouldering his shotgun, he turned and walked toward the cabin not looking back to see if Buck was following.

It was dark inside the cabin and the aroma of brewed coffee filled the air, awakening Buck's hunger. A hewed-log table and two benches took up the space left by a rope bed with a cornhusk mattress that was shoved against the wall. Several chickens scurried out of his way as Buck moved to one of the benches and sat down.

Without being asked, the man poured coffee into a cup and placed it before his guest. He reached up on a shelf and took down a tin. From it he took out some hard crackers and venison jerky. He gave these to Buck to eat.

Between bites and sips, Buck related the events of the previous night.

"Pirates, a curse on them!" the man spat on the dirt floor. "It's not only the high seas that knows the likes of them. They'd cut out their own mothers' hearts if there were a dollar to be gained in it. Lost men. Curse 'em, I say."

The man spoke with such feeling that Buck suspected he had had dealings with the sort.

"What kind of place do you have here?" Buck asked.

"A woodlot for the steamboats. I purchased the island early last year. Been cutting the timber and selling it as cord wood."

"That's hard work."

"Can't complain and I get a bit of company when a boat stops needing wood."

"How do you get your supplies?"

"A boy from the village brings them out regular-like in his skiff. And I got the dog. His name is Jack. He's good company."

At the mention of his name, the dog moved closer to his master and wagged his tail. Buck marveled at the transformation. Where was the killer that confronted him only moments before?

To pay for his meal, Buck helped the man split cordwood for most of the morning. Menklin tried to convince Buck to stay on for a month or two.

"I'll pay you as good a wage as you could hope to make in town," he said, "Fifty cents a day and all you can eat."

But cutting and splitting wood wasn't for Buck, and Menklin knew it, so he let the matter drop. In the early afternoon, three short blasts of a whistle announced a steamboat's intention to come into the landing to purchase wood. It was a large and handsome boat, and as it drew near Buck could discern her name in fancy letters painted just below the wheelhouse. She was christened the *Leslie Adams*.

"She's a regular customer," Menklin said as he started for the landing with Buck and Jack hurrying to keep up. "Captain's name is Breen. He's a decent, God-fearing man. He might take you along with him."

"But I have no money. The boatmen took everything."

"A big strapping boy like you? He'll find a use for you, don't you worry."

And so it proved to be. The woodcutter put in a good word with the captain who agreed to let Buck work off his passage. Buck's first job was to help tote the wood from the island to the boat. After that he was told to report to the wheelhouse. By the time he got there, the *Leslie Adams* was making five knots down the river. He had never been inside the wheelhouse of a proper steamboat, and to gaze out of the windows upon the water and surrounding countryside from such a height was an experience he would remember for the rest of his life. It took his breath away. The captain, observing his reaction, laughed.

"You've had a time of it by all accounts, young man. I want you to help the cook in the kitchen. We carry both freight and passengers. The freight doesn't eat but the passengers make up for that. What did the flatboatmen take from you?"

"A belt with three silver coins sewn to it, a purse containing twenty dollars in gold coins, a set of dueling pistols, and a fiddle."

"Dueling pistols? How was it you carried dueling pistols with you?"

"My mother gave them to me for protection."

Captain Breen was a kindly man and refrained from pointing out the obvious.

"But it was the loss of my fiddle that distresses me most," Buck continued. "It was not a valuable violin, but it was my first and I am very fond of it.

Captain Breen had kept his eyes on the river during this exchange but now he turned and studied Buck more closely. "You say you know how to coax a tune out of violin?" he asked.

"You could say that."

"How well do you play?"

"It's not for me to brag, but I did win a contest a couple of years ago. The prize was three silver dollars."

"And those were the coins sewn to your belt, am I right?"

"Yes, my mother sewed them on."

The captain smiled. "I've never won a contest, but I too play the violin," he announced. "Being the captain of a steamboat like the *Leslie Adams* can test your nerves. Dangers are legion: a sunken log can rip the bottom right out of your boat, or a stuck valve can cause the boiler to explode, blowing you and your passengers to Kingdom come. A flood can leave you high and dry in a cornfield two miles or more from the river. That is why I find playing the fiddle both a stimulating and comforting pastime."

Turning to his cub, Breen said, "Mr. Wright, if you would be so good as to take the wheel, I will return shortly."

The cub, a red-haired youth, leapt to his feet and placed his hands on the wheel that was nearly as tall as he was.

Without another word of explanation the captain left the wheelhouse. He returned in a moment holding a violin case.

He placed the case on the map table, opened it, and withdrew the instrument. Handing it to Buck, he said, "Please, be so good as to play us a tune."

The tune Buck chose to play was *The Lady's Waist Ribbon*, a tune similar to another called *Folding Down the Sheets*. Leaving the violin in standard tuning, Buck performed the tune flawlessly, playing the low part in the key of D and then switching to the key of A for the high part.

Captain Breen was delighted. "You'll not sweat in any kitchen on my boat, my boy. Just play for the guests after supper each evening in the salon and your passage is paid in full."

"But I don't have a fiddle of my own. The rivermen took it," Buck said.

"Then you shall use mine! As captain I spend so little time in my cabin I fear my violin suffers from loneliness."

The two and a half weeks Buck spent on board the *Leslie Adams* were some of the happiest days of his life. He and Captain Breen became close friends and on the rare occasions when the captain could free himself from his many responsibilities, Buck taught him fiddle tunes. *Three Forks of Sandy*, *Big Sciota*, *Going Down to Cairo*, and *Natchez Under the Hill* were Buck's favorites that had to do with rivers and river towns, and he was delighted to teach them to the riverboat captain. There are older men who resist learning anything from a younger man; they feel it is below them. Not so the good captain. In fact, he was so pleased with his "lessons" as he called them, he offered to take Buck on as a cub and teach him how to become a river pilot.

"If you can steer your way through the shoals and rapids of a breakdown playing the fiddle, you can learn to pilot a riverboat," the captain assured him. "What a pilot needs most, a sight more than boldness and an air of authority, is a first-rate memory. And you must have a good memory, Buck, or you could never remember the thousands of notes that go into making up the tunes you play. So, what do you say? Shall you be my new cub when Mr. Wright leaves me at the end of the year?"

Buck said he would think on it. He knew it was a generous offer and he would be a fool to turn it down. But the pull of music was as strong in him as the current of the river. Piloting a steamboat was a full time occupation. He saw that watching Captain Breen go about his day. Besides, there was so much more of the world he wanted to see before settling down to a set occupation. New Orleans was but one destination. From there he could sail around the Horn to California or visit the Sandwich Islands. He could explore China if he wanted to, like Marco Polo. His teacher in school owned a well-thumbed copy of the *Travels of Marco Polo*, which he often read to his students.

As they made their way south, eventually leaving the Ohio and entering the Mississippi at Cairo, the *Leslie Adams* stopped at numerous towns and settlements to unload or take on cargo and passengers. Sometimes the crew would take a jaunt around town and Buck would tag along. A visit by a riverboat, especially one as grand as the *Leslie Adams*, occasioned much communal merriment among the citizenry of the town. They gathered at the levee like a murder of crows, hungry for any scrap of news that might connect them to the larger world beyond the fields and woods that bordered their small hamlet. Fiddlers and banjoists would appear as well, looking to extract a few coins from the crowd of curiosity seekers. Perched on cotton bales and nail kegs, they sawed and plunked away and Buck would sometimes join them.

Once he convinced Captain Breen to invite a gang of the musicians onboard and they had a roaring good time playing tunes together on the starboard top deck with a large and appreciative audience packed together on the levee below.

At long last the steamboat reached Memphis, where they would tie up for a week before continuing downriver.

"The mayor of Memphis is an old friend of mine," Captain Breen told Buck once the mooring cables were let out and the boat pulled up snug to the shore. "His name is Eustice Hammerling and we went to school together. He and his wife are hosting a small gathering at their home this evening and he invited me to join them. I asked whether you might also come along. Like me, Eustice is a music lover and I told him that you play a fine fiddle.

"I appreciate the invitation, Captain, but perhaps I should remain on the boat."

"By my word, you are as strange a creature as any jackalope. This is not Parkersburg, son, but Memphis and proclaimed by many to be the finest city on the river next to New Orleans."

"I heard Vicksburg is a city worth visiting."

"I'll say it is—but why are we arguing over the merits of one river town over another? Why won't you accompany me to the party at the mayor's residence? I doubt you'll be offered an opportunity like this again for a very long time."

Buck looked uncomfortable. He stared down at his shoes.

The captain suddenly laughed. "Lord forgive me for being a numbskull but I do believe I know what your problem is. You're worried because you don't have the proper clothing to attend such a high-toned event."

"The river pirates took everything but the clothes on my back," Buck stammered.

"And they meant to have your skin, too, but you showed them." Breen turned to his cub. "Mr. Wright, you are much the same height and stature as our young Mr. Sullivan; would you be so kind as to lend him appropriate attire for this evening? I would be much in your debt."

Thus it was settled. As evening descended upon the city, the captain and his young companion strode down the gangplank and made their way through the bustling streets of Memphis, Buck carrying the captain's fiddle case. After a dozen blocks they turned a corner and climbed a steep grade before reaching an impressive white mansion with a columned veranda in front, overlooking the broad sweep of the river. The house was ablaze with light and inside they found a gay company of men and women of the first order. Mayor Hammerling was rotund and all the happier for it. His daughter, Wilhelmina, by comparison, was a slender willow, a shaft of moonlight, a stately crane with emerald eyes.

When a servant rang a bell for the guests to enter the dinning room, Wilhelmina sidled up to Buck, slipped her arm into the crook of his, and asked him to escort her to the table. Buck nodded. He did not trust his tongue; his surprise was too great. They joined the parade of guests.

Throughout the dinner, Wilhelmina laughed and chatted, flirted and demurred, whatever was necessary to remain the center of attention, which, as the only daughter of the mayor, was both her right and responsibility.

Following supper, Buck, at the urging of Captain Breen and his friend the mayor, performed for the assemblage. He played a march and a waltz and then the guests formed up for a dance, and the rest of the evening was spent cavorting. There were even times when the captain deigned to take over the fiddling so Buck could dance with the mayor's daughter.

Just past midnight the party came to an end and the captain and Buck prepared to leave.

"We shall hire a coach to take us back to the boat," the captain said, his mood, fueled by wine and good company, was such that no extravagance was beyond his reach.

Buck too had enjoyed himself and suspected he had fallen in love. As the carriage bumped along on its way to the boat, Buck considered leaving the *Leslie Adams* so that he might dally a while in this beautiful and fascinating city.

Early the next morning, Buck received an invitation for afternoon tea at the big house on the hill. He arrived to discover he was the only guest. Wilhelmina and her mother had the slave girl serve them on the veranda. The aroma of jasmine and magnolias filled the air. The whistle of steamboats drifted up the hill like the cries of exotic birds. They ate rainbow cakes served on hand-painted porcelain plates imported from Austria and they sipped scented tea grown in the kingdom of Siam. Had someone predicted that only three weeks after leaving home Buck would be surrounded by such luxury and entertained by a lovely young woman and her mother, he would have thought them crazy. And yet here he was. Life could surprise: be it the cruelty of river pirates or the sweet attentions of a goddess.

But upon on his return to the levee, he was caught up short by the sight of a flatboat moored downriver from where the steamboats were laid in one next to the other. There was no mistaking the boat or her crew. Buck ducked behind a stack of barrels of pickled herring that had traveled down from Minnesota. From this hiding place he could observe Captain Barlow and his men. They were busy loading large sacks of grain. His blood boiled. These were the very men who had intended to kill him.

After several minutes he grabbed his chance to slip away unnoticed. He ran to the city hall and asked to see the mayor. Mayor Hammerling was keenly interested in Buck's story, and he summoned the constable.

"Dale, take a detachment of militia and follow this young man to the levee. He will point out a flatboat. Bring the crew here. Use force if you have to, but under no circumstance let them get away."

The constable nodded. He was a tall man, his hair close shorn, and the small finger on his right hand was missing, perhaps the victim of a knife or bullet. Buck was confident the lawman was more than a match for Barlow and company.

"As for you, Buck," the mayor said, "don't let the boatmen see you. Once you have pointed out the flatboat, skedaddle back here fast as a hare. I want to prepare a surprise for the rogues who served you so poorly."

Thirty minutes later, the constable and three militiamen boarded the flatboat. Three more militiamen stood guard on the shore, each holding a rifle with fixed bayonets.

"Who is the captain of this boat?" the constable asked.

"That would be me," Barlow said, looking up from a ledger upon which he was marking each sack of grain loaded.

"The mayor of this city wants to speak with you and your men," the constable informed Barlow.

"What for?" Barlow asked. "We've done nothing wrong."

"He has a few questions to put to you. I trust you will come peaceably."

Barlow took in the situation at a glance: the constable and his men on the boat and three more on the shore, and any thought of resisting evaporated like dew on an August morning.

A short while later the flatboat crew and their captain stood before the mayor. They remained ignorant as to the reason they were summoned, because Buck, following the mayor's instructions, was hidden behind a heavy window curtain.

"You are here to answer questions," began the mayor who, as the chief executive of a bustling river town, had his fair share of experience dealing with rowdies and ruffians and brooked no orneriness or disrespect. "It is my understanding that you gave passage to a young man named Buck Sullivan this three weeks past."

Surprise, confusion and alarm washed over the faces of the five men. They looked back and forth at each other not sure who should talk first, the glint of panic unmistakable in each man's eyes.

The captain was the first to regain some semblance of composure, but his voice had lost its usual confidence.

"We did have a young man aboard our boat and that might have been his name."

"Was it his name or was it not his name?" the mayor demanded. Just behind him stood the constable, his eyes boring into those of each crewmember in turn until their guilt compelled them to turn away.

"Yes, I do believe his name was Sullivan or some similar Irish name. Maybe it was Mulligan."

"No, it was Sullivan, Captain," Curley piped up and Barlow whipped around with a look meant to knock his first mate to the floor. Then he turned back to the mayor.

"You see, your honor, the boy was crazy. Or he went crazy, it's hard to tell with such things."

"Explain what you mean?" the mayor feigned an attitude of genuine curiosity.

"Crazy, like the capt'n says," Curley joined in.

"Shut up, Curley," Barlow snapped. "I'll handle this."

"It was like this, sir," he addressed the mayor. "It was nighttime. We had just passed the mouth of the Wabash, a bad stretch of river for currents. The boy, Buck was his name, you're right now that I think about it, well, he jumps up like some old-time hell and brimstone preacher and starts ranting at the top of his voice. 'Repent! Repent! you worthless heathens or you will burn in hell!' Well, we're not used to being preached at as a rule and my men were bothered and I feared they might do some mischief to the boy, so I told him to pipe down. But he kept at it and that's when I see he wasn't quite right in the head. I even offered him some whiskey, hoping that might calm him down. So he takes a big gulp and then flaps his arms like a fighting cock, crows like one, too, then he jumps overboard. Just like that. We yelled for him but never got an answer. Curley grabbed a torch and held it out over the side but there was no a sign of the boy. As I said, the current is a killer through that stretch of river and can pull a strong man down in just a minute or two. I reckon that's what happened to the boy. It's a shame, really, him being so young and all."

The mayor marveled at the heartfelt way Barlow related his story. Had he not known better, he might have been tempted to console a man who possessed such deep feelings for a youth he hardly knew.

"Have you ever known a cottonmouth to crawl onto your boat, Captain?" he asked.

"I call 'em water moccasins, your honor," Barlow answered, his keen eyes trying to read the mayor's face for some hint as to the reason behind the question.

"Well then, do water moccasins ever climb onto your boat?"

"Now and again one will slither onto the boat after we've tied up along the shore someplace."

"Do you consider the water moccasin a dangerous snake?"

What was this all about? Barlow wracked his brain for an answer. The mayor is no fool. He first asks about the boy and then starts in about snakes.

"Its bite has killed more than one man," Barlow answered.

"Yes, you are right there," said the mayor. "And what do you do when you find such a loathsome and dangerous creature on board your boat or on the shore nearby?"

"I kill it," said the captain and his men nodded their heads in agreement.

"But why not just drive it away? Must you kill it? Is it not, after all, one of God's creatures?"

"God's creature or not," rejoined Barlow with feeling, "if I should fail to kill the snake when I have the chance, then am I not guilty if it bites someone else and causes his death?"

"Well reasoned," the mayor said with a smile. "Wouldn't you agree, Mr. Sullivan?"

Buck stepped out from behind the curtain and the effect upon the boatmen was akin to seeing a ghost.

"God save us," Curley blurted out. "He's alive!"

"Yes, very much alive, and no thanks to you," said the mayor and his eyes were now cold and stern.

A strange transformation came over Barlow's features, moving not from alert caution to fear of punishment but to a mirthless, resigned amusement. He shook his head and turned away from Buck to fix his attention on the mayor.

"So what are you going to do with us?" he asked.

"By your own judgment, you have judged yourself," the mayor said. "But you are altogether worse than the lowly snake. It does no more than obey its nature. You, on the other hand, are men, or were at one time, and as such have been given the gifts of reason and moral understanding Yet, you went ahead and betrayed this young man's trust, meaning to murder him in cold blood for the sake of a few trinkets. By so doing, you have forfeited your liberty, and perhaps your lives."

The mayor turned to the constable. "Take them away and keep them under lock and key until they stand trial."

The constable and his men led the boatmen from the mayor's office. The last in line was Barlow, and as he reached the door he turned to look back at Buck. Once more he shook his head and the constable, bringing up the rear, shoved him forward through the door so that he followed his crew.

Buck never forgot the look on Barlow's face at that moment. He should have felt satisfaction that the captain was brought to justice, but instead he felt only pity for a wasted life with all hope for redemption gone.

Later that afternoon when the flatboat was searched, the constable found Buck's belt with the silver coins, his money pouch, and the matched set of dueling pistols. Buck feared the rivermen had burned his violin or cast it overboard, but it too was recovered.

THE *Leslie Adams* departed Memphis three days later, but Buck was not on board.

"The river binds together all those who love it," Captain Breen said, shaking Buck's hand. "I'm sure we shall meet again."

"And when we do I hope you will have some new tunes to teach me."

This made the captain smile, and they parted friends.

At the trial Buck gave his testimony. The constable provided an inventory of the stolen items discovered aboard the flatboat. Under determined questioning by the prosecutor, Curley broke down and gave a detailed account of the theft and attempted murder. He was certain they would be found guilty and sentenced to death, and the image of the gallows took such hold of his imagination that he began to weep openly and had to be removed from the courtroom. Captain Barlow showed no remorse and gave only cursory answers to the prosecutor's questions.

The jury rendered their verdict without leaving the jury box. They found Barlow and his men guilty of robbery and attempted murder. They did not, however, bring in a verdict of piracy, which carried a mandatory death penalty. Accordingly, the judge sentenced the men to twelve years of hard labor. Two days later, just before they were to be transported to the state penitentiary in Nashville, a jailer discovered Captain Barlow dead in his cell. He had hung himself with his belt rather than face the claustrophobic constraints of a prison cell after so many years living free upon the river.

Buck remained in Memphis for two months before purchasing passage on a steamboat bound for New Orleans. He looked forward to seeing the ocean for the first time. He promised Wilhelmina he would return, and she promised to wait. His last act was to press upon Mayor Hammerling the set of dueling pistols.

"But these are quite valuable," the mayor objected, although his eyes betrayed his desire. "You should keep them."

"I owe you, Sir, for bringing those bad men to justice," Buck assured him. "Besides, I am a minstrel and must travel light. The treasures of this world are only a burden to me. Please take them. You are a rich man and know how to keep such treasures. They will not harm you as they would me."

Time passed and Buck returned to Memphis and married Wilhelmina. The mayor hired him to work as an agent for his shipping business, which provided Buck with numerous opportunities to visit other cities and towns along the river. But then the war came, and, rather than fight, Buck and Wilhelmina and their two young children traveled by ship to California. Settling in Sacramento, Buck became a successful wheat trader. He often longed to see his father, the river, but he learned to love his new home. He raised a large family. He continued to play the fiddle up until the day he died.

Now it is time to put aside our story and take a stroll together. Apollo's fiery chariot has dropped below the western rim of the world, the world is shrouded in darkness, and the stars have lost their shyness. Look there, to the north, just above the horizon. Can you see the Great Bear, what some call the Big Dipper? Now look to the south. Can you see the three bright stars all in a row? That is the belt of Orion, the hunter. Now I will tell you a secret. Sometimes when I scan the night sky and see those three bright stars, I think not of Orion, but of Buck Sullivan and the belt he wore on his first trip down the river, the belt with the three shiny silver dollars he won in a fiddle contest. And when I think about Buck and listen very carefully, I fancy that I hear his fiddle, playing up there in the heavens, the lively notes urging that great company of stars to dance and make merry.

MOTHER
AND
CHILD

Lester Tidewell found that he was growing increasingly dissatisfied with his lot in life. And according to the number crunchers in the actuary department of his insurance company, that life didn't have all that many years left on the clock.

"You haven't been yourself lately," Bernice said at breakfast one morning. "Are you unhappy with me?"

"No, you're as good a wife as any man could want."

"Then is it one of the children? They both have good jobs and we get to see the grandchildren whenever we want."

"No, it's not the kids. And it's not money. We don't live high like some folks, but we've enough to keep shame away."

"Then what's bothering you? Your mood is like the fizz going out of a bottle of soda."

"I can't rightly say," Lester said, pushing away his half-eaten plate of eggs and ham. The comparison with a bottle of soda had nettled him.

"I'm going out to the shop," he announced as he got up

from the table and grabbed his coat from the hook by the back door.

"A man is coming over from MacAlister this morning with a trunk load of student violins," he said. "There might be one or two worth buying."

"Maybe you need to take some vitamins," Bernice said as he jammed his hat on his head and started out the door. He didn't think he was a candidate for GERITOL quite yet.

A crust of icy snow crunched underfoot as Lester trod the path to the outbuilding where he did his fiddle trading and repair work. Why, he wondered, had he chosen such an oddball occupation for his livelihood? He already knew the *how* and *when* to the question. Born in 1920, the Great Depression rolled into his small town in southern West Virginia just as he was finishing up high school. His daddy was a foreman for the local coal company, and when the price of coal crashed the mine was shut down, and he was thrown out of work. Then the black lung put him in the miner's hospital over in Beckley, where he died the week before Lester's graduation. That put the kibosh on any hopes Lester had of going to college. One thing was certain though; Lester wasn't going to waste his life slaving underground and filling his lungs with coal dust. No sir. So he cast about for something else to do. He was good with his hands and found a job repairing mining equipment, but the stink of coal brought back too many hard memories. So he quit and went to work at a paper plant across the river in Kentucky. He bought a second-hand Studebaker and drove it home every other weekend to visit his mother and sister. During one of those trips, his friend Bobby Means, who had signed up to go into the army, gave him an old violin that had once belonged to his uncle.

"You keep it and learn to play," Bobby told Lester. "Or sell it, I don't much care. I aim to get me a pancake guitar when I save up enough money."

"What the heck is a 'pancake guitar?'" Lester asked.

"An electrified guitar. You plug it into an amplifier with a speaker. I read about them in *Popular Mechanics*. Electric instruments are the future and the future is where I'm headed."

Lester studied his skinny friend with his oversized Adam's apple and girlish hands and wondered how he would survive boot camp, let alone combat overseas, if it came to that. The Germans and Italians were on the prowl and Lester expected the United States to get pulled into a war sooner rather than later. He didn't think with his damaged heart—he suffered a severe bout of rheumatic fever when he was ten—that he would have to go, but a war was bound to change everything.

Then he met Bernice at a dance and they began stepping out together. They discovered, however, that they were different kinds of people. Where he was talkative and enjoyed pulling practical jokes, she was shy and quiet. He liked a drink now and then, but she was a committed teetotaler. All the same, she was willing to put up with him learning to play the fiddle, and that is saying something. So they got married on a Thursday and the following Sunday the Japanese bombed Pearl Harbor. The war, as Lester feared, had finally come to the United States, and most of the men he worked with went and joined up and they had to close the paper mill. Lester and Bernice moved to Michigan where he got a job making wooden patterns for bomber parts at Willow Run, and Bernice spent her days on the factory floor installing machine guns into belly turrets. At night when they weren't listening to war reports on the radio, Bernice sat in the front room of their small company house flipping through *Reader's Digest* or knitting while Lester sawed away on the fiddle in the bathroom with the door closed.

As the months passed, Lester's playing improved to the point where he felt comfortable enough to join a trio of musicians, each too old to serve in the military. The men met every Tuesday after hours at Hal's Barbershop, and in between playing tunes they swapped jokes and told stories. When he first started fixing instruments, Lester couldn't remember, but word got around and people began showing up at his house with broken mandolins, guitars, and violins, and he worked on them. The extra money was helpful, because Bernice had to stop work to have their first child, little Kenny. Then came Peggy and Clarissa.

At last the war came to an end and life rolled on and in the early 1960s, a month after John Kennedy was shot and killed, Lester decided to quit his regular day job and devote himself full-time to repairing musical instruments. He liked working on violins the best. There was just something about that unique instrument that took hold of his imagination and wouldn't let go. He was especially fond of its graceful shape, the delicate *f* holes on each side of the bridge and the way the scroll wrapped back into itself, like some of the seashells he picked up on the beach as a kid when his parents took him to see the ocean. Those were great times, going to the seashore. He remembered how good it felt to breathe in the salt air and listen to the soft pounding of the surf and the way the sand warmed the soles of his feet. Maybe a vacation by the ocean was just what he needed to get out of his funk.

He unlocked the door to the shop and built a fire in the woodstove using crumpled up newspaper, an empty egg carton, and a handful of pitch-laden pinecones. With the fire crackling, he hung up his coat and hat and picked up the violin he had left on the workbench. It was a Hopf, not a real Hopf, but a decent factory-made copy. Along one side was a row of clamps he had used to glue the top to the ribs where they had come loose. Lester checked the joint before methodically loosening each clamp. He hoped to get $300 for the violin now that it was repaired.

As he unscrewed the clamps, he realized a good deal of his dissatisfaction with life was the fact that after forty-four years fixing and dealing in violins, he had never gotten his hands on a truly great violin. He had bought and sold many fine instruments, but never a Stradivarius or Guarnerius or Amati. This never used to bother him. He considered himself more a fiddle trader than a proper violin dealer, a man who spent his summers driving from one bluegrass and old-time music festival to another, setting up inside a school gymnasium where the fiddle contest took place or else peddling fiddles out the back of his truck on the fair grounds near where the musicians hung out and jammed. But lately the desire to own a great violin had grown strong in him. It was as if a wizard or witch had cast a spell over him. Maybe it started when a fiddler named Clive Stalnaker died and his heirs decided to include his fiddle in the estate auction. Lester and Clive weren't close, but their paths had crossed many times over the years and Lester knew Clive owned a decent fiddle, although Lester never worked on it. The instrument possessed a dark warm tone, unlike many fiddles that when strung with steel-core strings have a bright tone but can sound strident. So Lester decided to attend the estate sale even though that meant driving three hundred miles there and back. In the hour before the start of the auction he checked out the violin as best he could, but there was no label inside and not much to go on. Then when the violin came on the block, Lester found himself bidding against a portly man wearing a tweed sports jacket and a yellow tie. The man hadn't bid on any of the other objects for sale that day, but every time Lester placed a bid on the violin, the man would top it. Pretty soon it was just the two of them with the price going up and up. Lester had two thousand dollars cash money on him and never dreamed he would need that much to purchase Clive's violin. In fact, he planned to stop in Huntington on his way home and look at a violin a librarian wanted to sell. But the bidding was already at eighteen hundred dollars and the man in the sports jacket showed no sign of quitting.

So Lester decided to go for broke. "Two thousand dollars," he shouted, hoping the jump from fifty-dollar increments to two hundred would drive the competition away. Instead, the man yelled out, "Twenty-five hundred."

Well, that did it. Lester knew Clive's violin was a good one, but he wasn't going to risk that much money on it. So he motioned with his hand to let the auctioneer know he was out of the running.

Lester heard later that the man who beat him was a violin dealer from Cleveland, and that Clive's violin was made by a Frenchman named Vuillaume. The dealer wound up selling it to the first chair of the Cleveland Philharmonic for nine thousand dollars. That was in 1970 and ten years later the loss of the violin still left a bitter taste in Lester's mouth. How much higher would the dealer have gone in the bidding? Did he know the violin was an original Vuillaume, or was he just guessing? And how did a country fiddler like Clive acquire such a valuable violin in the first place? So many mysteries.

Thus did Lester's thoughts wander as he laid each loosened clamp on the workbench. A violin was made from sixty-nine or seventy separate pieces of wood depending on whether the back was made from a single piece of wood or two pieces book matched so the flame in the maple radiate out from the center seam, and Lester knew each part as he did the notes of his favorite fiddle tune, *Ragtime Annie*.

A car pulled up outside and Lester went to help the music teacher bring in the violins. There were twelve violins, four violas, and a cello. The strings program had been cut at MacAlister Middle School, and Mr. Harding, the music teacher, was hoping to recoup some money for the district before he retired. Why are so many good things being lost, like music and art in the schools, Lester mused as he stacked the instrument cases along the wall farthest from the woodstove. Is it because we keep spending all our money fighting a bunch of stupid wars?

"It'll take me a while to evaluate this many instruments, Bill. Can you leave them with me for a couple of days?"

The music teacher agreed, and Lester began repairing a sound post crack in a violin that belonged to a taxidermist.

When Lester peddled his fiddles at festivals he laid out an assortment of instruments on a table beginning with the less expensive violins on the left, those in the $50 to $200 price range, to his best instruments on the right, which might fetch as much as $1,500. That way beginners and experienced players had something to choose from.

"It's not an exact science," he would tell someone inquiring about the worth of the violin or bow they were interested in. "What is it worth to *you*? That's the important question."

This sometimes got the person miffed.

"You know more about these things than I do. You tell me what it's worth."

"Here's how I do it," Lester would beam a smile, the best way he had learned to deal with an obstinate customer. "You tell me how much you're willing to pay for a violin and then I'll lay out a selection that will be in your price range. None will be over what you can spend and a few might be quite a bit less. It doesn't matter. You try each violin and, if one speaks to you, if you find yourself coming back to it over and over again, well, then that's the fiddle you're meant to have. That's when I'll tell you how much it costs. Now you've got to admit, that's fair."

Some people liked this way of buying an instrument; others didn't. The latter was the kind of person who feared purchasing the wrong kind of fiddle because he didn't know enough about violins to tell a good one from a bad one, and it was that fear that kept him from trusting his own ears and the way the fiddle made him feel when he drew the bow across the strings. So he would move along to the table of the next violin dealer, where each instrument had a price tag hanging from the scroll like the price tag Minnie Pearl dangled from the brim of her straw hat when she performed on the Grand Ole Opry. In other words, the $100 and $800 price tags on the violins calmed the customer down and put things in perspective.

Sometimes the most difficult part of being a fiddle trader was when someone came up to you with a fiddle they wanted to sell.

"This belonged to my grandmother," they would say. "She played in the orchestra in Moline, Iowa. It says inside that it's a Stradivarius."

And Lester would have to explain that many violins had stickers inside with the name STRADIVARIUS printed on them, but all that meant was that the violin was made in the Stradivarius style. Often they would refuse to believe him, might even accuse him of trying to cheat them out of a genuine treasure. Or if they *did* believe him, he saw the wind come out of their sails and that wasn't fun either. For years they had believed that if times ever got lean or they wanted to take that around-the-world trip, all they had to do was sell grandma's old violin. Whether angry or discouraged, they most often walked away and sold the violin later to another trader who told them the same thing. To Lester it was just a variation on the old kill-the-messenger routine.

Some days Lester wished he had gone to school to become a psychologist instead of toiling his life away as a lowly fiddle trader. He knew as much about how people think and act as any psychologist and yet they made heaps more money than he did selling violins.

One day while driving his truck to the Old Fiddlers' Convention in Galax, Virginia, he took an inventory of how many fiddles and bows he had bought and sold over the years. He had a notebook on the seat next to him, and every time he thought of a transaction, he would make a hash mark with a pencil. There was that first fiddle Bobby Means gave him that he later sold to a sheriff's deputy in Winchester, Virginia. Then he bought six violins at an estate sale in Connellsville, Pennsylvania. The deceased was an avid collector of musical instruments, and his house was crammed full of violins, mandolins, autoharps, accordions, banjos, and hammered dulcimers. After that there was a nervous man who came to him with a trunk full of violins. No sooner had Lester opened the trunk and reached in to grab one of the cases, than the man pulled back his leather jacket so Lester could see the handle of a SMITH AND WESSON sticking out of his waistband.

"Why are you showing me a gun?" Lester asked, pulling his hand away from the instruments.

"In case you're thinking of offering me a check. I only take cash," the man said with the look of a hunted animal in his eyes. Lester wondered if he had stolen the violins, but he wasn't about to ask.

"Well, what will you give me for 'em?" the man said.

"I need a few minutes to check them out."

Lester laid the fiddle cases on the ground and opened each one in turn, examining the violin inside. But they were all junk, or so busted up that the repair bill would be more than they were worth.

"I think I'll take a pass on these violins," Lester told the man. "They are not exactly what I'm looking for."

He didn't know how the man would react, and was relieved to see him shrug and then zip up his jacket.

"You're making a big mistake, mister," the man said, shaking his head like Lester was the village idiot. He then loaded the violins back into the trunk of his car, placed a pinch of snuff in his mouth, and drove away looking for someone else to buy his trunk full of worthless violins.

As the miles slipped under the tires of his truck, Lester added more and more hash marks to his list. He knew he was forgetting lots of trades, but he was surprised he remembered as many as he did.

Yes, it was funny kind of life, a small profit here, a loss there, and then drive ten hours just to check out a violin or deliver a bow. And when he wasn't on the road, he would often stay up far into night fitting a set of pegs and a new bridge. At first Bernice went with him to the festivals, but she never cared for crowds, so she would find an excuse to stay home. Lester missed her company but he understood.

And it wasn't like he was going to run away with another woman. His violins were his women, shapely creatures with narrow waists and ample thighs and sometimes there was one with a voice so sweet and pure it made his heart sing.

Still, in all that time, he had never owned, even for a week, one of the very special violins. The dealers in the cities who sold violins to the classical music crowd were the fortunate souls granted that privilege. Not the Lester Tidewells of this world.

Now time had caught up with him and he was going to have to give up the trading soon, at least the traveling part. He would keep tinkering with violins, but he knew age would begin easing him out of the trade. It was this thought that nagged him day and night; his chance was gone. Maybe there was something to the idea of reincarnation, he sometimes wondered. If you don't get what your heart desires in this go-around, you get it next time. Otherwise, how could you explain where the desire came from? Something planted the desire in his heart. Was it God? Perhaps. But even though he prayed to God for a satisfied mind, this request had not been granted.

The winter passed and in August Lester and Bernice rented a two bedroom apartment a block from the water in Ocean City, New Jersey. The sea breezes provided a welcome change from the hot and muggy weather they were having at home and they whiled away the time titled back in beach chairs getting sunburned and watching young girls flirt with the lifeguards. At night they strolled the boardwalk, stopping to sample the fudge and salt water taffy. Once or twice, they played miniature golf and Bernice won a free game when her ball went straight up the ramp into the hole of a tree where it then popped out and hit Rip Van Winkle on the head and he sat up and stretched. They laughed at that, but still the "black dog"—the name Lester gave his depressive mood—nipped at his heels.

One morning as he was getting ready for the beach, Bernice told him she was going to the hairdresser's.

"You go on your own," she said. "I'll be back by lunchtime."

The weather was warm but the sky was overcast and there were few people on the beach. He decided to walk south, away from where the boardwalk ended to where a series of sand dunes separated the summer homes from the beach. His thoughts drifted like dandelion seeds upon the air, until he realized that he had succeeded in forgetting all about violins and bows and the other traders who now peddled cheap Chinese-made instruments. This made him smile. He was on vacation, his first vacation in a long time, and he meant to enjoy it.

Then he noticed a small child building a sand castle. The child was by himself, he was maybe seven or eight years old, and he was using a shovel to scoop up the sand and pour it on the walls and towers of his castle. Only as Lester drew near, he saw that it wasn't a shovel. It was a violin with the top missing, the boy holding it by the neck with one hand and pushing sand into it with the other. Why it hadn't fallen apart with such usage was a puzzle to Lester but he went over to have a closer look.

"That's a fine castle you're building, young man," he said to the boy.

The boy looked at him but didn't say anything, his face a riot of dark freckles.

"What's your name?" Lester asked.

"Billy," the boy said.

"How old are you?"

"I'm seven."

"Where are your parents?"

The boy pointed with the violin at a bungalow just beyond the dunes. It was yellow with bright blue trim and it had a large picture window facing the ocean.

"Would you let me look at your shovel? It's a violin. Did you know that?"

The boy nodded and then handed the violin to Lester. "I couldn't find my shovel," the boy said.

"Where did you get this one?" Lester asked but his attention was divided. He was inspecting the inside of the violin, the garland of ribs and the way the linings were perfectly inset into the corner blocks. The workmanship was exceptional. He turned it over and examined the back. It was made from a single piece of quilted maple and there was a half circle of ebony surrounding the button, which meant the neck had likely been reset some time in the past. The purfling was flawless as was the carving of the scroll. Then he noted the neck graft joint where the neck met the peg box. That might indicate the violin was made before 1800. After that, the necks of violins were lengthened, the bridges were raised, and the bass bars extended in order to make the instrument louder. This was particularly necessary for soloists who needed to be heard in large concert halls.

But what most impressed him were the lines of the violin. To Lester who had looked at tens of thousands of violins over the years, there was about this violin some ineffable quality in its simple and yet elegant proportions that brought pleasure to his eye and warmth to his soul. He was certain a true master had made the instrument.

"Can you tell me where you found this violin?" he asked the little boy. He was perspiring even though he wasn't hot.

"Mommy found it in the attic. She said I could use it." He held out his hand for the violin and Lester had to force himself to return it.

"Would you do something for me?" he asked.

The boy looked at him but didn't say anything.

"Would you take me to your house so I can speak with your mother?"

"But I'm building a castle."

"It will only take a moment. Maybe your mother will let me buy you an ice cream cone." There was a snack stand not far down the beach and Lester pointed to it.

"Okay," the boy said and he jumped up, his little legs and knees caked with sand.

"Bring the violin with you. Somebody might come along and step on it."

The boy carried the violin as he led Lester across the dunes toward the house.

Lester's thoughts flowed like the phrases of melody: the violin is a superior instrument, maybe not one of the great instruments, but a violin worth a great deal of money—*if* the top can be found.

The distance to the house was not far but the anticipation made time draw out painfully.

"Here we are," the boy said as he climbed three steps onto the small porch, pulled open the screen door, and ran inside, letting the spring hinges slap the door shut. Lester listened as the boy called his mother. "There's a man to see you, Mommy."

In a moment a woman came to the door, the boy just behind her. She was wiping her hands with a large plaid dishcloth, and she wore a sundress decorated with printed flowers. Her expression was pleasant, not suspicious, which made everything easier.

"Good morning," Lester began. "My name is Lester Tidewell. I'm a violin dealer. I was walking along the beach and saw your son using the back and neck of a violin to build a sand castle. I was wondering where he got the violin."

"We bought this house a year ago," the woman said, "and we found the violin when we cleaned out the attic."

"Who owned the house before you?"

"A man named Huntger. He lived in New York City and spent his summers here in Ocean City. I never met him. He was eighty-five when he passed away. I don't think he had any family. A realtor friend of mine in the city heard about this cottage and knew I was looking for a summer place and I was able to purchase it before it was listed."

"Was Mr. Huntger a musician?"

"I don't know. I think he came to the United States from Europe just after the war. That's all Patty told me about him. That's my friend, the realtor."

There was a moment of awkward silence. Lester wasn't sure what to say next.

"You can have the violin, if you want," the woman said, and this startled Lester.

"But I need it for my castle," the boy whined.

"I'm sure we can find your shovel," the woman said. "If not, I'll buy you another one.

The boy appeared only partially mollified by this offer. He came around his mother and pushed the screen door open just enough to slip out onto the porch. He gave Lester a quick look before hoping off the porch and wandering around the side of the house, kicking the sand as he went.

"Is there any chance that you have the top for the violin?" Lester asked the woman.

"I believe so," the woman said. "I think the heat in the attic must have melted the glue. You're welcome to come in, Mr. Tidewell, if you wish. I'll have to go upstairs and look for it. I think it's still in the violin case."

Lester entered the house and waited in the living room as the woman went in search of the rest of the violin. Lester looked out at the ocean through the picture window and tried to image the sun rising red and majestic above the blue of the water, the renewing light filling the room. He was recalled from this daydream by the sound of the woman's steps drawing near.

She entered carrying a carved violin top in one hand and the case in the other. The sight of her nearly stopped his heart.

"I thought it was still with the case," she chirped. "Do you think it's a good violin?"

"I think it's a very good violin," he said, struggling to find his voice. "I'm not sure who made it. There is no label, and if there was, it's fallen out. May I look at the top?"

She handed him the piece of spruce. He held it up to his nose and smelled it before moving it near the window so he would have more light. Like the rest of the violin, it was skillfully carved and then he noticed pencil writing on the inside of the right upper bout. The words were very faint and his eyes weren't up to the task.

"I think it is an old violin and was made in Italy."

He looked more closely at the woman. He noticed that she wasn't wearing a wedding ring and he wondered if she was married. She had a pleasant manner and her eyes were kind. All the same, he sensed a deep sadness about her. Was the boy her only child? Who was the father? He wanted to know more, but he didn't think it was his place to intrude.

"I don't have any money with me," he said, "but I would very much like to buy this violin, if you're willing to sell it. I could come back later, with the money, I mean."

He was stumbling on his words, which seldom happened when he was trading.

"Oh, you don't have to *buy* it," the woman said with a smile. "You can just *take* it."

He was trying to figure out what to say and before he could speak, she continued, her words falling upon his ears like soft water over smooth stones.

"What I mean, Mr. Tidewell, is that the violin is all in pieces and I don't know the first thing about violins. I played the piano for several years as a child, but I'm not what you would call "musical."

"But I would like to buy it." Lester said. "I believe it could be quite valuable." The trader's voice inside his head tried to scold him. "Don't tell her that. She'll want to too much and you don't even know what it is worth."

But some deeper instinct warned Lester against listening to that voice. "I'd be happy to offer you three thousand dollars for the violin. I would just need time to draw the money from my bank."

This made the woman laugh. "You surprise me, Mr. Tidewell. Three thousand dollars *is* a great deal of money. But to be honest with you, money no longer means very much to me. So please, take the violin. If you hadn't come along I'm sure my son would have destroyed it."

"Would you at least let me offer you a thousand dollars?" Lester asked. He had never begged someone to take more than they asked for. What was happening to him?

"If it would make you feel better, yes, I will take a thousand dollars. But I'm sure that's far more than the violin is worth."

"Then we have an agreement," Lester said. "I will draw the money from my bank today and pay you in cash."

"You can write a check if you want," the woman said.

"My checkbook is back at the apartment."

"Good. Then just take the violin with you and drop off a check later."

"Are you sure?" Lester felt as if he were in a dream. He might wake up at any moment.

Then he noticed the woman's eyes. They were blue with flecks like gold and they regarded him with genuine affection.

"It's always wonderful when someone finds what he is looking for," she said. "I wish you only good fortune with your new violin."

And that was that. Lester placed the pieces of the violin inside the case and carried it back to the apartment. Bernice was still at the hairdresser's, so he wrote a check for a thousand dollars and walked it over to the yellow house with the blue trim and gave it to the woman. Two days later he and Bernice said farewell to Ocean City. Bernice remarked several times on the way home that it was the best vacation they had ever taken. Lester agreed although the last two days had been a torture for him. He wanted so much to examine the violin, take photographs of it and send them to experts he knew. He wanted to see how difficult it would be to glue the top back onto the body. Check the top and back for cracks. Some cracks were hard to see. But he was on vacation and so he forced himself to leave the violin in its case. It had waited a long time, a hundred years or more, so it could wait a few more days. He owed that much to Bernice.

"May I speak with Mr. Francais?" Lester asked the young woman behind the counter. It was Lester's first visit to the Jacques Francais Rare Violins Shop. He had called earlier and scheduled an appointment with the owner, a world-renowned expert at evaluating violins.

"He's in the back," the woman said. "I'll see if he's available."

A moment later Mr. Francais appeared. He was older than Lester expected but his eyes sparkled with intelligence and good will.

"How may I help you?"

"My name is Lester Tidewell. I called last week."

"Of course. May I see the violin?"

"The top is separated from the body," Lester said.

The appraiser spread a red velvet cloth on the counter top and then laid the two pieces of the violin on the cloth. For several seconds he merely looked at them without saying a word. He then picked up the top and held it out at arms length to judge the proportions. He put it down and picked up the rest of the violin and as he did a few grains of sand spilled onto the red cloth. Mr. Francais smiled and then he held the violin out and rotated it slowly, his gaze keenly focused on the subtle curves and recesses and quality of workmanship.

Returning the violin to the counter he drew out a loupe from his pocket and fitted it to his right eye. He then picked up the top once more, turned it over, and read the faint pencil writing on the inside.

The city outside could hurry along as much as it needed to: anxious drivers jockeying to get across an intersection before the light changed, cabbies blowing their horns, two elderly ladies having a spirited conversation in Yiddish as they walked down the street; but inside, the violin shop was a chapel of tranquility where beautiful polished instruments, many a hundred years old or more, hung by their scrolls in neat rows, each with its own unique voice and character, waiting patiently for just the right player to come in and take it home.

After what seemed many minutes, although it was but a few, Mr. Francais rendered his verdict, and no man in the dock ever waited with greater anxiety than did Lester Tidewell at that moment.

"When we spoke on the telephone, Mr. Tidewell, you thought the violin was Italian. I agree with you. It is also quite old."

"Can you identify the maker?"

"Unless I'm very much mistaken, this violin was made by Giovanni Battista Guadagnini."

Lester knew what that meant, and the news did much to quicken his pulse. He had never seen a Guadagnini, but he had read enough about the Italian makers to know that Guadagnini violins, although lesser known than those made by Stradivarius and Guarnerius, were viewed by some experts as every bit their rival. In fact, some of the best violinists in the world played Guadagnini violins.

Lester felt lightheaded and considered sitting down.

"According to the pencil writing, this violin was made in 1775," Mr. Francais continued.

That's over two hundred years ago, Lester thought to himself, the year of Lexington and Concord and the beginning of the American Revolution.

"During the years Guadagnini made violins," Mr. Francais was warming to the subject, a note of excitement entering his voice, "he lived in four different cities in Italy: Piacenza, Milan, Parma and Turin. Given the year, this violin was made in Turin and those are considered his finest because by then he was a fully mature maker. I would say you are very fortunate to possess such an exceptional instrument."

"Is there a chance it is just a copy?" For some obscure reason Lester felt a compulsion to disprove what he was being told.

The appraiser gave a small shrug. "It is possible but highly unlikely. I have looked at thousands of violins during my career and you develop a kind of sixth sense for the genuine article. All the same, there are tests that can confirm what I believe."

"But how badly damaged is the violin?"

"Not much. It's been repaired in the past, but the work was done with skill. As for the top, I just think the glue failed. It should be a fairly simple procedure to glue it back on. It will also need a new sound post. Would you like us to make the repairs?"

Lester pulled into the driveway as dusk was settling and the lights were going on in the houses up and down the street. He left New York at five in the morning to beat the traffic and stopped only for gas and a quick lunch. He felt stiff as he walked from the car to the back door. Bernice was in the kitchen preparing dinner.

"Well, what did you find out?" she asked after he had hung up his coat and hat. "I thought you would call?"

"I guess I needed time to think."

"Well twelve hours on the road is plenty of time for that. What was so important?"

"The violin. It was made by a man named Giovanni Battista Guadagnini."

"That's some name," Bernice said smiling. "I wouldn't want to have to spell it."

When Lester failed to smile at her joke she said, "Is he somebody special?"

"Yes, very special."

"So where's the violin?"

"I left it with Mr. Francais to restore."

"How much will that cost?"

"Four hundred dollars."

"Couldn't you have done the work?"

"Maybe, but I didn't want to."

"Are you hungry? I could fix you a plate."

"In a few minutes. Come into the living room, we need to talk."

"Why not talk to me in here. You seem, I don't know, so serious. Are you not feeling well?"

"I'm fine. I'm better than fine," he said and then smiled in a way Bernice had not seen him smile in years, not just with his lips but with his eyes.

"Let's go in the living room," he said and she followed him.

"Do you want a drink?" she asked. "You must be bushed."

He nodded and she went to the sideboard and poured two fingers of bourbon into a glass. She went back into the kitchen, added a splash of water and a couple of ice cubes. Then she poured herself a glass of sherry and carried the two glasses back into the living room.

"Okay," she said handing Lester his drink, "tell me all about Mr. Guadagnini. What did the appraiser tell you the violin is worth?"

"He could only guess."

"So are you going to make me guess?"

"No." Lester took a sip of his drink. "Mr. Francais said that, once the instrument is restored, he could, by making one phone call, find a buyer willing to pay $400,000 for the violin. Given more time, he might find a buyer willing to pay even more."

The news took Bernice's breath away and she dropped unto the couch nearly spilling her sherry. After she had collected her thoughts, she asked, "Did this Mr. Francais offer to buy the violin?"

"He said the shop would broker the sale if I wanted and take a percentage. As I said, he knows people who would be interested."

"I thought only Strads were worth that much money?"

"A Guadagnini is right up there with them. Mr. Francais said my violin is a 'masterpiece.' That's the word he used."

Lester finally settled himself into a chair.

They both sort of stared off into space for half a minute, leaving their drinks alone.

Finally Bernice spoke.

"So what are you going to do?"

"The question is what are *we* going to do?"

"We should sell it."

"Yes," said Lester, but his voice was flat.

"And that would make us rich," she continued, tentatively, as if feeling her way into the future that awaited them. "Not like a Rockefeller or Onassis, but we could go on a world cruise. We could buy a larger house. We could help the kids."

Lester nodded but to Bernice he looked like a man under a sentence.

"You don't want to sell the violin, do you?" she asked.

"I've turned that question over and over in my mind for the last twelve hours. I've never owned a violin this special, haven't come close. I used to dream I would one day, but I gave up that dream years ago."

"So you've waited most of your life for this to happen, and now it has."

"It appears so."

"Then why aren't you over the moon?"

He took a long pull on his drink before answering.

"I am happy, incredibly happy, but there's something I have to do first."

"You want to keep the violin. I can understand that. I mean we don't *need* the money. We're comfortable enough and we'll soon have my pension and your social security. And we have a little saved up. If it makes you happy to keep the violin, then just keep it."

"It's not that simple; I wish it was."

Now Bernice was confused.

"Do you want to sleep on it and talk in the morning?"

"No, we might as well talk about it now."

Bernice knew she was missing something, but what? For the life of her she couldn't imagine what it was.

"You mentioned our savings," Lester said. "How much do we have?"

"Twenty-eight thousand dollars give or take a jar of pennies. We had more but we gave Peggy and Jim $2,500 three months ago to help them with the down payment on the house they wanted to buy."

"How much do we need to live?"

"All of it."

"That's not what I mean. If I continue buying and selling

fiddles and you work another year before you retire—you want to keep working, don't you?"

Bernice nodded her head. She was a school secretary and loved being around kids.

"Okay, then, in a year you'll start getting your pension and I'll get social security. So how much of a financial cushion do we need to keep us from being anxious?"

Bernice ran her fingers through her hair; it was difficult question to answer.

"Ten thousand, something like that. What is this all about, Lester?"

"I need to give more money to the woman I got the violin from. I need to give her as much as I can. It won't be enough. It won't be anywhere near what the violin is worth, but I need to do this."

"Why? Why do you have to give her more money? From what you told me, she wanted to *give* you the violin. She would have allowed her boy to break it or leave on the beach. You don't owe her anything."

"I know. Strictly speaking, I don't owe her the money, but I need to give her some money. It's something I have to do if I want to feel that I truly *own* the violin. You know the parable of the ten lepers?"

Bernice nodded although she was having trouble making the connection.

"Well, Jesus cured all of them, right? He made them clean. But then only one of them came back to thank him and that's the one Jesus blessed."

Bernice studied her husband. This was a side of his nature she rarely saw. He wasn't an outwardly religious man. He seldom went to church, even though she went most Sundays. And here he was quoting scripture.

"I think it's more like the parable of the merchant and the pearl," she said, "When the merchant found the pearl of great price, he sold all that he had and used the money to buy it."

Lester nodded but didn't say anything.

"And if for some reason we just had to have money?" she let the question hang in the air.

"If one of us got sick or the children needed our help?" Lester asked.

"Yes, that's what I mean," she said.

"Then we would sell the violin. No question about it."

"But for now you want to keep it?"

"I would love to. At least for some months—maybe a year."

"Then we will keep it as long as we can. Will you play it?"

"Sometimes, but that's not why I want to keep it."

"I realize that."

She took a sip of her sherry. "Lester, you've been a good husband. You work hard, you don't waste your money on drink or foolish schemes. So if you really want to do this, then it's okay with me. Would fifteen thousand be enough for the woman?"

"Yes."

"Do you have her address?"

"No, but I should be able to find it. I know her name and when I went back and gave her the check for the violin she mentioned she lived just outside Philadelphia. She said she was a teacher at a private girls' school."

"Well, you take a day or two and get rested up, and then you go find her and give her the money."

"Don't tell anyone about the violin, about how rare and valuable it is. And we should insure it. Of course, we'll tell the children in case anything happens to us. But no one else."

Bernice understood. If word got out they owned such a violin, dealers and musicians would be on their doorstep morning, noon, and night. And there would always be the threat of being robbed. At their age the last thing they needed was that kind of worry.

"What about the people in New York?"

"Mr. Francais assured me that he wouldn't tell anyone about the violin unless I asked him to. I believe he is a man of his word."

"When are you driving back to New York to pick it up?"

"It should be ready by next week."

Lester went over and sat next to her on the couch. He took her hands in his.

"Are you okay with this?" he asked her. "No new house? No world cruise?"

She looked into his eyes and she could see that his spirit was whole and he was at peace. She would do nothing to take that away from him.

"You must play the violin for me when I've had a bad day at work. And on Sundays when I get home from church."

Lester nodded and smiled and continued cradling her hands.

Lester found the woman and gave her the money, despite her objections. He also bought Billy the largest ERECTOR set he could find.

"It has a small electric motor, Billy, so you can make an operating crane or a drawbridge. You can't use it on the beach, but I know you like to build things."

"This is swell. Thanks."

Lester hung the Guadagnini on the wall of his shop where he would see it every morning when he came in and before he set to work regluing a base bar or fitting new tuning pegs on a copy of a Stainer. Some mornings he took the violin down and played *Those Endearing Young Charms* and the notes filled the room with magic and set his own soul singing.

Thus the next seven years were the most contented years of Lester's life. He had found what he most desired, and the fate of the violin, after he died, was for his family to decide.

Lester passed away in his sleep seven years to the day after he came upon the child on the beach. Over the years he often thought about the boy and his mother.

Eventually the Tidewell family decided to sell the Guadagnini violin. It was purchased by a syndicate of investment bankers for the princely sum of $1,475,000 and is currently being played by a twenty-four-year-old Russian violinist who won the coveted gold medal at the International Fritz Kreiseler Violin Competition last year.

And so may we all, like Lester Tidewell, find what we most desire and be content.

Two Sisters

"The convicted murderess, Miss Edith Turnbull, daughter of retired United States Senator William Clarke Turnbull, mounted the steps of the scaffold at seven o'clock this morning with an air of quiet dignity. Her unadorned prison garments fashioned of gray cotton cloth did little to detract from her great beauty. The Reverend Cecil P. Allenson, pastor of Christ the Shepherd Church, accompanied the condemned from the cell to the scaffold, reading the blessed words of Holy Scripture for the comfort of her soul. Never before has this reporter observed a crowd gathered to witness an execution so subdued. Some openly wept as the noose was fitted around the young woman's neck and the black sack pulled down over her head. An assemblage of women who had positioned themselves in the yard near to the scaffold began singing the hymn *Nearer My God to Thee*, their plaintive feminine voices rising in the still morning air to such effect that all conversation ceased, leaving only the birds in the trees to chirp their greetings to the brightening day, ignorant of the sad event taking place nearby. Then prison warden Superintendent Clay O'Neil read the decree of the court. The words fell hard on the ears of those in attendance. A man yelled out, "Serves her right," upon which cruel utterance a scuffle broke out and several men had to be removed by constables. Then, when all was in readiness, the trap door was sprung and young Edith Turnbull was given over to the ages."

~ Vernon T. Jupps, special correspondent, *The Tennessee Star*, May 18, 1860

I will attempt to put down on paper as near as I can a chronicle of the tragic events that led to the untimely deaths of Edith and Elizabeth Turnbull. Edith was born in 1837 to William and Mary Turnbull. Her sister, known affectionately as Beth, was born two years later. At the time, William Turnbull was a successful lawyer in Knoxville. A decade later, he won election to the United States Senate representing the great State of Tennessee.

The two children grew up in a comfortable and well-ordered household. I can say this with assurance for I was, for many years, a frequent guest in the Turnbull home, having been William Turnbull's law partner and later his political advisor. In appearance and temperament, the two sisters could not have been more different. Edith was dark haired and dark eyed. Her younger sister, Beth, had hair the color of wheat and eyes blue as a June sky. Edith was passionate and strong willed, virtues in their way, but for her often a source of bitter frustration, which is often the case with such women who must content themselves with living in a man's world.

Beth was sweetness itself. One could not resist bringing her little treats and dallying a while in her company. She was a fanciful storyteller as well, who loved nothing better than talking about the fairies that lived in the flower garden behind the house.

The mother, Mary Turnbull, I am sad to say, was a woman in thrall to ambition. Early in her marriage she decided that her husband was destined for great things, and it was her task, since he seemed to lack sufficient ambition, to make sure he received the renown that was his due. If this resulted in her becoming the wife of an important United States Senator with duties that included entertaining the leading citizens of the country, well, so be it. And should her husband be elected president, there was no telling, in Mary Turnbull's mind, where destiny might lead them. These were her thoughts as she packed up the house in preparation for their move to the nation's capital.

I know the girls welcomed the elevation in the family's situation. Washington was far more engaging than dreary old Knoxville. At their school, they not only rubbed shoulders with the daughters of other senators and congressmen but also with the daughters of ambassadors from foreign countries.

As the two sisters grew into young womanhood, I cannot testify as to whether or not they remained close. I cannot recall an instance when a harsh word passed between them, but I doubt propriety would have permitted such an exchange to take place in my presence. The real trouble, however, began when Senator Turnbull hired a young man to serve as his private secretary.

Mr. Steven Wilcox was strikingly handsome and possessed the twin gifts of charm and vitality. As such, he wielded a powerful influence over women. They were drawn to him. They loved him. They entertained fantasies of running away with him. Not only maidens felt this way, many a married woman had her head turned by this youthful Adonis. My own wife, Mildred, bless her soul, was so smitten by the dashing Mr. Wilcox that for some months she would blush whenever he entered a room where she was. This irritated me at first, I must admit, but when I perceived Mr. Wilcox played no part in her childish infatuation, was not only innocent of eliciting this response, but totally unaware of it, I found my own affection for the young man deepen. But such heroes, and that is what he was, can bring destruction when thrown in among mere mortals, whether they mean to or not. So it proved for Edith and Elizabeth. They both fell hopelessly in love with their father's secretary. Both meant to have him for her very own and looked to her own gifts to win in love's competition. With Edith, that was her intelligence and beauty, and she engaged Wilcox on the issues of the day whenever the opportunity presented itself. The war that would tear the nation apart was as yet some years in the future, but already lines were being drawn.

"What should be done about California?" she would ask Steven. The wealth pouring into the economy from the gold fields of California was shifting the balance of economic power increasingly in favor of the northern states with their banks and manufacturing capabilities. Where would this leave her native state of Tennessee? And had he read the transcripts of the Lincoln-Douglas debates?

Wilcox was deeply interested in politics and found these discourses with a thoughtful, attractive woman much to his liking. But it was Beth's innocence and soft ways that in the end captured his heart. They began to walk out together and everyone expected that an engagement was imminent.

Then one day Edith invited her younger sister to go on a picnic with her. Beth was distressed by the growing animosity between her and her sister occasioned by their rivalry over Steven Wilcox, so she eagerly accepted. They drove a one-horse shay west several miles skirting the southern bank of the Potomac before stopping on an isolated high bluff that overlooked the river. There they spread their blanket on the grass and enjoyed cucumber sandwiches and lemonade while the horse awaited its return to the stable.

Throughout the afternoon the sisters talked about the old days in Knoxville and the close friends they had left behind. The sun made its descent and Beth grew slightly chilled and began packing up to leave.

"Stay just awhile longer," Edith urged her. "I brought you here to show you something very special."

"What is it?" Beth asked.

"Come with me to the edge of the bluff; it is almost time."

Beth followed her sister to where the ground dropped sharply away and a rock-faced cliff fell thirty feet to the flowing river below.

"Now look west up the river. See?"

Beth looked and marveled at how the setting sun

transformed the river into a shimmering, crimson ribbon. She had no inkling of her sister's foul intention until she felt the shove that sent her tumbling over the edge and down into the river.

Beth survived the fall, but the impact with the water badly jarred her senses. As she came sputtering to the surface she called out to her sister because she did not know how to swim. Edith yelled down to her, "I'll not save thee and lose for all time the man I love. He shall be my husband, not yours."

Beth sank a second time, the sinewy, cold fingers of death grasping her legs and pulling her under. But she fought back and won the surface and cried again for help.

"I renounce him. Marry him if you wish. Only save me, for I am drowning."

But Edith would not be moved. She stood with arms crossed and watched as death had his way, pulling Beth beneath the small rippling waves.

Edith set about staining her dress with mud and tearing it in two places. She then returned home bearing a tale of woe. Beth, she told her parents, had slipped and fallen into the river. Edith jumped in after her, but already it was too late. She cried for help, but no one came to her aid. She walked the bank of the river until darkness made searching impossible.

The Senator and his wife were beside themselves with worry. The senator sent Steven running to find men willing to help search for his daughter. Several hours later in the dark of night, twenty men gathered below the bluff, each holding a torch, and they began working their way up and down both sides of the river while the anxious parents called their daughter's name over and over again. "Beth! Beth! Where are you?"

Late the next day, the search was called off, and Senator Turnbull and his wife returned home to accept as best they could the loss of their fair-haired daughter. But the grief engendered by that loss proved a heavy burden to bear.

Everyone was so fond of little Beth, most of all, the youthful Steven Wilcox. He was so distraught, in fact, that he could not eat nor sleep. Unable to concentrate, he offered to resign his position, but Senator Turnbull would not hear of it.

"The sorrow will pass in time, Steven. Go visit your family. They will be a comfort to you. I can manage."

Steven did spend several weeks with his parents and siblings in Philadelphia, but his heart still ached when, at the end of the month, he returned to work. And as the days passed, he found himself turning more and more to Edith for solace. Sometimes they took long walks together, and he found in her a trusted confidante, someone with whom he could share his feelings of loss and loneliness.

"I understand, Steven," she told him. "Beth was my dear sister and I miss her terribly."

Thus encouraged, Steven asked Edith to be his wife. The Turnbulls gave their consent and all that remained was to pick the right moment to make the announcement.

Whether or not Edith felt remorse or shame for what she had done, I wish I could say, but I cannot. If she had such feelings, she kept them under lock and key in a secret chamber deep inside her mind, far from prying eyes. Necessity was her sole master now. She had done what had to be done. She must live in the present, not the past. It was time to attend to her trousseau.

Return now to the scene of the crime. While it is true that no human eyes other than those of the cruel sister saw the unexpected shove that sent Beth tumbling over the edge of the cliff and into the river, and no human ears other than those of the cruel sister heard Beth's anguished pleas for help, there *were* eyes and ears: the eternal eyes and ears of an all-knowing and loving God, who, as the Master teaches us, "Are not two sparrows sold for a farthing, and one of them shall not fall on the ground without your Father?"

So Beth's body did not remain lost. Instead, it was carried by the current many miles downriver, past fallen timbers and jutting rocks, avoiding sand bars and eddies, until it came at last to rest against the dam of a mill race. The mill belonged to Horace Symington, a middle-aged widower, and in the morning as he prepared to start the mill turning he noticed something white several feet below the surface of the water, pressed against the face of the dam. But it had rained the day before and the water was murky so he could not make out what it was.

"Must be a dead swan or a lamb," he said aloud as he trudged back to the mill to fetch his hook and line.

He tossed the hook just upstream so that it floated down to the dam face. He yanked the rope, but whatever was on the other end was heavier than he expected, the rope straining his fingers. Spreading his feet, he leaned back and worked the rope hand over hand until, with a slosh of river water, Beth's body broke the surface. Symington was so surprised, he momentarily let go of the rope, but then he grabbed it, the rough hemp fibers digging into the palms of his hands, the momentum wanting to tumble him into the water. He took a deep breath and set his feet again. Blood throbbed in his temples. Slowly he worked the rope until he succeeded in pulling the body onto the grassy bank. Beth's white summer dress was streaked with reddish mud and her hair was a mass of tangles, bits of twigs and leaves caught in her long tresses. Her face was white as the moon and her eyes were open, staring up into the morning sky.

Symington felt his bile rise and was about to be sick. He turned away and took several long breaths to give his stomach time to settle. He then turned back to the corpse of the young woman.

Who was she? How old was she? What accident had befallen her? How long had she been dead? His agitated state of mind turned like the mill's large wheel, lifting each question in turn from the rushing, mysterious river of fate.

He reached down with his thumb and index finger and gently closed her eyes. Her cold flesh cried out for the warmth of life, and he was filled with a depth of sadness he had not known since the day his wife died. This young woman was sorrow itself, and he had to wipe the tears from his eyes.

Time passed and he knew he should fetch the sheriff but some force bade him to linger. The young women's features were so pure and innocent; even in death her beauty smote his heart. He began picking the twigs and leaves from her hair. He had never felt hair so fine. Then he noticed a ring on her right hand. It was gold with an emerald stone; a gift, had he but known it, from the young woman's parents on the occasion of her eighteenth birthday. Symington touched the ring and felt an odd thrill. He turned the ring, and it slipped from the finger as if by its own will. His heart was pounding. He held the ring up into the sunlight, the precious stone flashing green and timeless. A second shiver passed through him, and he stuffed the ring into his pocket. He cradled the young woman's hand in his own. It was so light and delicate, like the body of a bird, the bones thin and elegant.

Something very strange was happening to Symington. He was falling under a spell. Time passed without awareness. The river gurgled as it flowed by, indifferent to the tragedy.

Besides working as a miller, Horace Symington played the fiddle. He was quite a decent fiddler, in fact, and he spent most of his weekends making music with a small orchestra in a nearby town. It was upon this part of his nature that the spell sought to work its magic. He imagined he heard a melody floating upon the air, a melody full of sadness but also possessing a poignant, bittersweet beauty.

How can anyone describe what happened next? To even contemplate it causes a shudder. Symington was not a deranged man, although he began to act like one. Gazing at Beth's lifeless body, the thought came into his mind that he should bury the girl's body and tell no one. Even stranger, he should remove several of her finger bones before burying her body. The finger bones he should then fashion into tuning pegs for his violin. He should also cut strands of her long golden hair and weave them into the horsehair of his bow. This way her spirit would pass into his instrument, so whenever he played she would live again.

Symington flicked open his pocket knife and set to work. A red-tailed hawk cried far above the rustling river, as it swept its way east toward the bay and the ocean.

A month before the Tennessee Democratic convention was held in Nashville, Senator Turnbull announced his decision not to seek reelection but to return to Tennessee and take up the practice of law again. He made the announcement during an interview with a reporter from the *Daily Evening Star* without first consulting his wife, an oversight that caused him some misery.

"You said what?" Mrs. Turnbull demanded, barely able to contain her fury.

"I told the reporter that I am leaving the Senate."

"But the presidency was within your grasp. All you had to do was reach out and take it."

They were in the library of their Washington home, and a warm summer rain pelted the panes of the French windows.

"The next president will be a Northerner, or a westerner with Northern sympathies," Senator Turnbull told his wife. "Even if I managed to get nominated and go on to win the election, being president would be the worst job in the world. This republic of ours is for the scrap heap. Those of our fellow citizens who would drive us apart will have their way. Can't you see that?"

"All I see is a weakling, a man who never really wanted to make a difference and who found an excuse to give up in the death of his daughter."

William Turnbull seldom raised his voice in anger but his wife had gone too far.

"Be quiet, woman!" He walked to the French window and he looked out into the gray sadness and tried to regain his composure. After a moment, he turned and spoke.

"What you say has some truth in it. Losing Beth made me reconsider my priorities. I spent so little time with her because of politics. Instead, I wasted my time on craven office seekers, political hacks, and mean-spirited newspapermen."

"But Beth would have wanted you to become president," his wife said, the fight far from out of her.

Turnbull stifled a laugh, and then shook his head sadly.

"No, Beth wouldn't have wanted that. Edith does. She's like you. The fire of ambition burns white hot inside of her."

"And what's wrong with that? Is it because she's a woman? Should she be meek and mild? Well, let me tell you this. Edith has more sand than ten of you!"

Steven Wilcox entered the library at that moment as the Turnbulls turned away from each other, fuming. He too was reeling from the news that the senator was retiring. What should he do now? Return to Philadelphia? Move to Tennessee? Or should he remain in Washington? Edith loved the capital, the parties and the intrigues.

"I'm sorry to disturb you," he said, "but Secretary McWalters is here to see you, Senator."

"Tell him I'll be with him in a moment," the senator replied.

As Steven left the room, he heard his future mother-in-law's voice rise in indignation.

"Why I wasted my life trying to help you make something of yourself, I'll never know. If I had only listened to my mother. . . "

It was decided that the Turnbulls would host a lavish party, the grandest Washington had seen for many years. It would be their way of saying goodbye to their many friends and announcing the engagement of their daughter Edith to Steven Wilcox.

For the event they rented the Willard Hotel and hired the city's leading caterer. They also contracted the services of a concert orchestra under the baton of Simon Kennedy to entertain the guests and provide music for dancing.

A week before the gala event, either by coincidence or the hand of Providence, Kennedy decided to visit his uncle who was the mayor of a small town located several miles west of the capital. The uncle had arranged for the local

orchestra to perform a benefit concert for veterans of the
Mexican war. The lead violinist of the orchestra was Horace
Symington and Kennedy was moved by the sound of the
miller's violin.

"Your violin has remarkable tone. Quite exceptional.
Would you consider selling it?" Kennedy asked Symington
while the orchestra was taking a break.

The question appeared to unsettle the miller.

"No, I . . . I would never sell this violin," he stammered.

Kennedy was not surprised. If he owned such a violin, he
would never sell it. "What can you tell me about the maker?"

"Very little, I'm afraid. There is no label. I bought it from
a man who went bankrupt speculating in railroad stocks."

"Well, I don't believe I've ever heard a violin to match it."

"It's not suited to all music," Symington said.

"What do you mean?"

"Well, you can play any kind music on it, from marches
to quadrilles, and it sounds good. But the more melancholy
the tune, the more its tone grabs hold of you. It is hard to
explain."

"The tone does have a plaintive quality to it, to be
sure," Kennedy said and then he refilled his cup from
the punchbowl. "Do you have any obligations for next
Saturday?" he asked Symington.

"Nothing pressing," answered the miller.

"Good. I would like to hire you for a special event that
will take place at the Willard Hotel. One of my violinists is
suffering from the grippe. If you can read music, you could
take his place."

"I can read music, but I seldom travel that far."

"I will pay you handsomely because the family hosting
the event is generous beyond what is customary."

"Why is that? Why are they so generous to musicians?"

"The Turnbulls are an old Tennessee family and they are generous to everyone. It is their going-away party and an engagement party for their daughter. What do you say? Will you not join us at the Willard and bring your fine violin along?"

The night of the grand party all of Washington high society was on hand: senators and congressmen, cabinet secretaries, and Supreme Court justices, along with the top military men. The president, who was in New York City dealing with Tammany Hall, sent his regrets along with a case of champagne to toast the betrothed couple. The gowns glittered like those imagined in fairy tales. Everyone knew the dark brooding clouds of conflict, possibly even civil war, were on the horizon, but for this one evening those weighty matters would be forgotten.

Symington arrived at the Willard in the early afternoon so he could rehearse with Kennedy's orchestra. The musicians were slated to entertain the guests as they arrived for the banquet and later they would move to the ballroom to provide music for the dancing. Thus as the evening began they were positioned to the side of the head table. They played the *Tennessee Waltz* as Senator and Mrs. Turnbull arrived with their daughter Edith and Steven Wilcox. Everyone in the orchestra seemed to be enjoying himself except for the miller. The aroma from so many flower arrangements made his head swim, and, even though he played regularly with an orchestra, he had never played with one as accomplished as Kennedy's. He had to struggle to keep up, which made him anxious, and he berated himself for agreeing to participate.

At a signal from the head butler, the orchestra ceased playing and waiters dressed as proper 18th century footmen emerged from eight mirrored doors that ran along one wall of the banquet hall, each balancing a large tray of steaming food. There were mounds of steamed Maryland crabs, haunches of tender lamb, roasted quail, steak and kidney pie, a feast that would have done Henry VIII proud.

As the guests consumed their last mouthfuls of apple dumplings and mince pie, Senator Turnbull stood to toast his daughter and her fiancé. The servers retired and the room quieted, except for a young man who shouted to his Aunt Matilda—the woman had left her ear trumpet at home—that the toasting was about to begin. This made everyone laugh. Then the contented guests turned their attention to their host.

In a rich baritone that had served him in the well of the Senate for many years, Senator Turnbull began his oration:

"My good friends, today is a special day for our family. We say goodbye to a city we love. But not with sadness. No, if leave-taking were our sole concern here tonight, then there would be sadness, for we love this city and its people and it grieves us that we should part. But this is also for us a joyous occasion because our lovely daughter Edith will soon wed the man she loves. She—"

A queer, unexpected sound arrested his words. It broke through the solemnity of the moment like the cry of a child and grew steadily in volume until all could hear it. Heads turned to find the source and there was Symington, the sound coming from his violin. The instrument lay on his lap, and he could feel it vibrating through the wool cloth of his trousers. He was panicky with bewilderment. The violin was playing itself, the notes rising up into the air without the agency of fingers or bow. Then the notes became a voice, a woman's voice, clear and pure and insistent. Now terrified, he wanted to knock the fiddle to the floor and stamp on it, break it to pieces, but he had lost command of his muscles. He was frozen in place, like Lot's wife, a pillar of salt.

A murmur arose among the gathered company but subsided as every ear bent to the words the violin sang.

> *There was a young lady, so gay and so free,*
> *Went with her false sister the sunset to see.*
> *High on a bank above a river so wide,*
> *Did stand and gaze as her sister drew nigh,*
> *And from behind, unseen, like cowards all,*
> *Did shove her fair sister and cause her to fall.*
>
> *With hungry water all swirling around,*
> *She cried for help before sinking down,*
> *Never to see the sun above,*
> *Nor hear the tender words of love,*
> *Or hold her child's hand and stroke his soft hair,*
> *And whisper in his ear his bedtime prayer.*
>
> *Alas, this raven-haired sister now sits and boasts,*
> *And with smug satisfaction is honored with toasts.*
> *For she now has the man she most adores,*
> *For whose sake did she her own sister abhor,*
> *Yet from her bed her lover shall flee,*
> *Knowing her now a cruel murderer to be.*

A stunned silence hung in the air following the last word of the song. Everyone turned toward the head table where sat Edith Turnbull and Steven Wilcox.

The Senator, stock still, looked at his daughter, his heart a battleground where indignation and doubt made war. "I don't understand," he stammered. "Tell me this cannot be true."

But Edith refused to look at him. Instead, she stared in front of her like a child entranced by a magic lantern show.

The Senator turned toward Symington, his rage slipping its leash.

"What kind of cruel prank is this? Who are you? Why are you doing this to my family?"

Symington blanched, not knowing what to say or do. Every eye was now upon him.

Then bafflement gave way to a halting realization and he found his voice. "I found her. A young woman. I didn't know who she was." Beads of sweat stood out on his forehead and he repeatedly clenched and unclenched his fists. "I'm a miller. The river current trapped her against the dam of the millrace. I swear to God above that I had nothing to do with her death!"

"Did you report this to the authorities?" demanded Bill Helbson, the city's chief of police, as he hurried around the table to prevent the miscreant musician from attempting to flee.

But Symington remained where he was, shaking his head dejectedly. "There was a ring on her finger. A gold ring set with an emerald. I buried her body and kept the ring. I know it was wrong."

Chief Helbson motioned for his deputy chief, a fellow guest at the banquet, to summon the police officers stationed just outside the hall, while he positioned himself next to Symington, a firm grip upon the fiddler's shoulder.

Suddenly a soul-wrenching wail filled the room. Everyone turned to look at Edith. She was standing, her eyes wide and terror-stricken, her cheeks a deathly white. Steven tried to take her by the elbow but she yanked her arm away as if his hands were fire. A moan came from the far end of the banquet table as the wife of Congressman Efferington fainted and was only saved from falling from her chair by the Swedish ambassador who managed to get his arm around her. Symington, meanwhile, began a rambling speech about a violin and bones and tuning pegs, about golden hair and a fiddle bow. Then he broke down completely and sobbed, his head in his hands.

A pair of police officers joined the chief, and, taking Symington firmly by each arm, they prepared to escort him from the hall. The chief took custody of the violin and bow and placed them back inside the case before Symington was led away.

The guests were now on their feet. Women gathered up their cloaks, musicians stowed away their instruments, and waiters scurried back to the familiar safety of the kitchen.

Steven Wilcox tried again to comfort Edith but she pushed him away before dropping back into her chair. She commenced pulling methodically at her hair, small fistfuls of raven black hair falling upon the white linen tablecloth, her face a mask of despair and damnation. Mary Turnbull was crying. The senator poured himself a glass of cognac and tossed it back. All was in ruins about him.

In the days, weeks, and months that followed the banquet, Horace Symington was charged with robbery and failure to report a death and sentenced to prison for eight months. Edith Turnbull became a mute; she would speak to no one. The only evidence implicating her in the death of her sister was the song of the violin, and no judge would allow that to be admitted into a court of law. This did not matter.

Indifferent to her mother's pleading, Edith wrote and signed a full confession. In it, she told of her love for Steven Wilcox and how she planned and carried out the murder, even how she ignored the cries of her drowning sister.

I did what I could to protect the family, but the newspapers were ravenous for the story. They hounded the Turnbulls wherever they went. The senator and his wife both longed to return to Tennessee, but they stayed for the sake of their daughter. Thankfully, they were spared the humiliation of a public trial; Edith pled guilty to premeditated murder. Many hoped the judge would be lenient and sentence Edith to prison, or even the madhouse. But the right honorable Rufus T. Mills, an acerbic man of Old Testament sensibilities, sentenced her to death by hanging, and Edith refused to sanction any lawyer to appeal the sentence.

Mary Turnbull begged her husband to use his influence with the president to have the sentence commuted to life imprisonment, but he refused. He had come to accept the fact that his daughter wanted to die. The senator and his wife formally separated a month after the execution, he returning to Knoxville and she to Nashville where her brother lived.

Steven Wilcox did not attend the execution. He moved to New York City three months after the banquet and took a position with a bank on Wall Street. Five years later he was made partner and married one of the richest women in the city.

So you now have the story. I was there when the executioner pulled the level that released the trap door. I thought Edith might say something at the end, a few words to unburden her heart and help prepare her to meet her Maker. But she refused to speak. She died with dignity and an air of resignation.

As for the miller's violin, it is now in my possession. I do not know how to play the violin and doubt I would play that enchanted instrument if I did. I keep it for reasons I don't quite understand myself. I will not sell it or give it away. But I will not destroy it. How could I? If only a portion of Beth's spirit resides inside the instrument, then I will do nothing to harm her spirit.

Once, during the last year of the war, I took the violin from its case. It was late at night, my soul was suffering the restlessness that comes with old age, and I could not sleep. I tightened the bow and drew it across the open strings. I pulled the bow slowly from one end to the other across one string and then I pushed it slowly across the next string. I was half-afraid the violin would begin to sing again, but instead I found the long notes soothed my heart. Then I had a vision. In this vision I saw Beth, young and fair and bathed in a golden light, embracing her dark-haired sister Edith. And the older sister's eyes were full of tears but also of joy, because the sisters were reunited and the jealousy and the crime were forgotten. That is the only time I dared play that violin, but often I wonder if what I saw that night was merely the yearning of my own heart or, perhaps, a true vision of that blessed realm that awaits us all, where Love is king and sweet forgiveness is ours simply for the asking.

Thaddeus Woodard Coplin, Esq. February 4, 1867

And down the road come a fiddler fair,
Bow down, bow down;
And down the road come a fiddler fair,
Bow down, balance me;
And the only tune that the fiddle would play was,
Oh, the dreadful wind and rain;
And I'll be true to you, my love,
If you'll be true to me.

SAY OLD MAN, CAN YOU PLAY THE FIDDLE?

Jason and his father did not get on well with each other. Neither was to blame; it is just the way things are sometimes between a father and his son, the father too ready to find fault, while the youth allows resentment to set up shop inside his heart for slights both real and imagined. So it was Jason's mother who came up with the idea that her son should take music lessons from a local fiddler. She hoped it would provide Jason with an opportunity to develop a more satisfying relationship with an older man, while getting the boy out of the house one or two evenings a week.

Thus on Tuesday and Thursday afternoons, Jason would jump off the school bus at Higgins Corner and walk up Dutch Run, the gravel road skirting the stream as it gurgled and splashed its way to the ocean a thousand miles away.

Ira Cockrill's farm was at the head of the holler and it took Jason twenty minutes to walk that distance. He then crossed a swinging bridge spanning the creek to reach the fiddler's house.

Ira, meanwhile, would leave off his chores and return to the house so he could brew up a pot of coffee and wait for his student to arrive. The old man had played the fiddle since before he could remember, learning his style of bowing and many of his tunes from his father, a well-known and respected fiddler in his own right. Ira never married and had no children of his own. A year earlier while in town, Cal Walker, Jason's father, stopped Ira on the sidewalk in front of the bank.

"Afternoon, Ira," Cal said, "how's the farm these days?"

"Could use more rain."

"Are you still playing the fiddle?"

"Can't see a reason to stop."

"Well, I was wondering. My wife thinks my son should learn to play the fiddle. Maybe you could give him lessons. I'd pay for the lessons, if you're willing."

The idea of getting paid to teach the fiddle intrigued the elderly musician, but he had reservations.

"What's the boy's age?"

"It's Jason, my oldest. He just turned twelve."

"Does he want to play the fiddle?"

"I don't think he's given it much thought."

"Then why pay for lessons?"

"It's Ruth's idea, like I said. The boy does like to sing. Ruth thinks he gets music from her side of the family. He sure as shooting doesn't get it from my side," Cal laughed good-naturedly.

"How much are you willing to pay?"

"You tell me."

"Well, let's see if your son takes to the idea first, then we can discuss terms."

Ira had never given formal music lessons and wasn't exactly sure how to go about it. Jason had his doubts too, but once he got a violin in his hands and learned how to draw the bow across the strings without it setting his teeth on edge, he was sold. Ira could tell the boy had talent and realized that teaching him would be more pleasure than chore.

That was five years ago. Jason was now a senior in high school and wondering what he would do after graduation. He was tall and good-looking and the best fiddler in that part of the state. There wasn't anything he couldn't do with a fiddle: make it sound like a lonesome train rolling through the mountains, a mockingbird singing from the top of a tree, a chicken laying an egg, even a mule braying at a heavy load. It seemed like every weekend he was off playing his fiddle for a dance, a wedding, or a house party.

Even so, he continued with his lessons, not because he believed Ira had any more to teach him, but because he was fond of the old man. And when his lesson was done, Jason would stay to talk or fill the old man's wood box or patch the garden fence to keep the rabbits out. He knew Ira's rheumatism was getting worse and he was having trouble managing the farm. Jason could also hear the decline in Ira's fiddling, but he never said anything about it for fear of giving offense.

Ira knew all the standard square dance tunes, but the way he played modal tunes was unique. *Shakin' Down the Acorns*, *Elzick's Farewell*, *Pretty Little Dog*, the melodies burst from his fiddle like a thunder of ruffed grouse breaking cover, catching the listener by surprise. Jason would know Ira's fiddling anywhere, even though the old man's left hand was failing and some of the notes had lost their clarity.

"Making music is about giving something of yourself," Ira would tell his young charge. "It's not the same as what a blacksmith does making a set of horseshoes, or a lawyer drawing up a will, or a miller grinding the farmer's corn. Those things are important and part of the business of life, the buying and selling of the provisions that keep us alive in this world. But a person can't eat music. You can't wear it like a coat to stay warm or enter it like a house to keep the rain off. Music is for the soul, not the body, and you've got to be careful with things that have to do with the soul. They are gifts."

The old man sipped his coffee before resuming his sermon.

"I've known my share of fiddlers over the years, and the truth is, Jason, God has given you a rare talent for music. It's a gift you've been given and it's your duty to share that gift with others."

"A duty?" Jason asked, genuinely puzzled.

"To whom much is given, much is required," Ira answered. "It's in the Bible. Luke 12:48. Now, I'm not saying people can't pay you a little something to play for them now and again. It used to be I got paid by the dance, a nickel a dance from each couple that was doing the dancing. But the music was still a gift that I was giving them. I know it ain't the easiest thing to understand, Jason, but if you want music to be a blessing in your life and not a curse—and, mind you, it can be a curse—then take what I'm saying to heart."

Ira would look intently at Jason after one of these lectures to see if his words hit their mark, but it's easier to peel a raw egg than to tell what a young person is thinking.

Jason did his practicing without being told, an hour or more a day. Then Jason graduated from high school and the lessons ended. He had no interest in college or in learning a trade. All he cared about was fiddling. He did, however, land a job with a natural gas company, traveling around the county checking on the company's gas wells and pumping stations. The pay was decent and he married a girl he had dated all through high school. Her name was Julienne. She was the daughter of a dentist who lived in town. She was also voted the prettiest girl in graduating class. Still, pretty or not, she was no fool, and she urged Jason to devote more of his time to his job and raising a family than playing the fiddle.

"You're gone every weekend playing music someplace. Why can't you spend more time at home? Don't I make you happy?"

Jason hated these conversations. He loved Julienne. Hadn't he married her? But fiddling was his life. Not just fiddling, but competing in fiddle contests. That really heated his blood. Some fiddlers got nervous before a contest; so nervous their playing went all to pieces. Not Jason. Competition spurred him to play his very best. And he loved winning. There was no feeling like it in the world, the way the other fiddlers looked at him after the head judge handed him the blue ribbon and the envelope with the prize money. He saw the envy in their eyes; they wanted to be *him* so bad it hurt. Girls too, they loved a winner, and sometimes they followed him out of the hall, angling for a way to hook his attention.

"Excuse me, but do you have change for a dollar so I can buy some chewing gum?"

Or "Are you related to the Walkers who live in Charleston? No? Well, you have the same nose. You really do. All the Walkers have the same nose. See, I've got a Morris nose. It's kind of short but it's cute, don't you think?"

And he might walk the girl home or take her to the ice cream parlor, or maybe they would hunt up a moonshiner, it all depended on the girl, and share a jar together. Now that was some fun.

A year after they were married, Julienne gave birth to a baby boy. A year later she gave birth to a girl. Jason got a promotion but with the promotion came a heavier workload, which cut into his time for fiddling. This made Jason irritable and he took it out on Julienne.

"Why do you have to drive all the way to Wheeling this weekend?" she asked one evening when he got home from work.

"I told you. There's a fiddle contest and the winner will get to play on the radio, on the Jamboree."

"But I told you that Momma's birthday is this Saturday, and you promised we'd go to my parents for supper."

"We'll go next weekend."

"Your supervisor called yesterday. He said you missed an important meeting."

"Did you tell him I was sick?"

"I'll cook your meals, Jason, and I'll wash your clothes, but I won't lie for you."

"Where do you think I was, if I wasn't at work?"

"That's not my business."

"You've got that right. My fiddling and what I do with my spare time is my affair."

The word "affair" made her ears smart. That is what she suspected. It all went together: the fiddling, drinking, and womanizing.

The baby started to cry and that ended the argument. While she nursed, she heard the truck start up and drive off. Well, she wasn't going to wait another week; she would go to her parents' house on Saturday, just her and the kids. Lord knows, sometimes she was tempted to throw his fiddle in the fire. But she knew that wouldn't change anything. He would just get another one and off he would go again. If he kept on like this much longer, she would, by God, get a divorce. She still had her figure and Buddy Samples who managed the supermarket flirted with her every time she went shopping for milk and eggs. He wasn't as good looking as Jason, but she could do worse. At least he was interested in her and wasn't a slave to the fiddle.

That Saturday Jason took first place in the fiddle contest in Wheeling. He drove back the next weekend to perform on the Jamboree. To his credit, he did bring his contest winnings home but thought Julienne should be more appreciative.

"It takes money to live in this world, if you haven't noticed," he told her. "And if I can make a little extra with my music, well I don't see what all the fuss is about."

"It ain't the money, Jason, and you know it!" she would fire back. "I swear you're away so much traveling for your job and going to contests, the kids'll grow up not knowing who their father is!"

These arguments only made Jason feel sorry for himself. He was an artist, couldn't she understand that? In this way resentment opened the door for pride and ambition to gain mastery of his heart. And like the writer who wishes another writer ill because his novel just made the bestseller's list, or the painter who takes no pleasure in his own work because the paintings of another artist hang in the museum, Jason Walker had to be the best at playing the fiddle. Some of the fiddlers he competed against he had known for years. Several had become close friends, or used to be. There was a time when after a contest he would join them back in their hotel rooms and they would play music and tell stories and drink whiskey until dawn sent them to their beds. Or he might spend time with a girl. Not any more. Now he went back to his room and practiced his music. He practiced at least three hours a day, and, if he slacked off for some reason, he knew it. Others might not, but he did. And if he could tell the difference, he allowed the judges could, too. So he kept at it, ignoring the cost.

His closest friend was a fiddler named Charlie Edwards, and Charlie had a signature tune he played in every contest he entered. It was a fine, complicated version of *Durang's Hornpipe* and Charlie more than once walked away with the top prize playing it.

So Jason decided to show Charlie up. He spent the better part of a winter perfecting his own version of *Durang's Hornpipe* so he could, as he often bragged to himself, "beat Charlie at his own game." He went so far as to copy, note for note, bow stroke for bow stroke, the most intricate passages of Charlie's rendition of the tune and then he added a shock of embellishments and complex bowing patterns of his own.

In the spring, he and Charlie were both entered to compete in a contest in Cumberland, Maryland. Charlie went first. He played his *Durang's Hornpipe* and the audience clapped and whistled when he was done. When Jason's turn came, he stepped out on stage and played his version of *Durang's Hornpipe*. There was no mistaking his intention. He aimed to show the audience and the world that he could play rings around Charlie Edwards and anyone else if he had a mind to. The crowd went crazy and he won the contest. But afterward, backstage, he was surprised when his old friend wouldn't speak to him. He heard later that Charlie gave up playing the fiddle, his taste for music soured. Try as he might, Charlie couldn't find a way to make it sweet again.

Jason shrugged off the whole episode with the excuse that Charlie was a sore loser. "If that's how he wants to be about it, then that's his lookout, but I aim to be the top fiddler in the country and nothing, or nobody, is going to stand in my way."

Competition fiddling is like college football in that it can be difficult to say for certain which fiddler, or team, is the best in the country when the season is over. A number of fiddle contests bill themselves as *the* National Championship. Given, however, that organizations such as the chamber of commerce and Elks Club sponsor the contests, it is wise not to put much stock in the claim.

So one year Jason set himself the task of winning all the big contests. That way there could be no doubt when all was said and done who was the *true* National Champion. It became an obsession with him, and he spent so much time traveling from contest to contest that his bosses at the gas company threatened to give him the sack.

He started out by winning a big contest in Asheville, North Carolina, and followed that up with another win in Dayton, Ohio. He then went south and won two more contests and finished the summer by taking first place in a contest in Kansas. That left only one more National Championship contest to win and that was held in Idaho.

Jason arrived at the convention center where the contest was to be held late in the afternoon. His back ached from driving twelve hours a day for three straight days, and he needed to get some sleep. But he paid his twenty-dollar entry fee and received his number. It was number 17, which pleased him because he had won a contest six months earlier with the same number. Two hours later the list of contestants was posted and Jason recognized many of the names. They had come in from every part of the country. Some were no more than teenagers, the up-and-coming young fiddlers that everyone was talking about, much as people once talked about him. A few of the contestants were women. A handful of the older fiddlers had been around the circuit for decades, seldom winning but always trying. These older men made Jason feel uncomfortable, although he couldn't figure out why. Perhaps it was how some of them hung out in the bars after a contest playing for drinks.

Jason took his supper alone at the hotel before making his way over to the convention center. Backstage, he found the other contestants milling around waiting for things to get started. Many were anxious, whether they showed it or not. They were thinking about what the audience and judges would think of their playing and half afraid they would mess up somehow. But Jason was true to form: calm and confident. His thoughts and will were focused on just one thing—winning. That was all that mattered. To be the best. Why else had he spend all those hours practicing until the joints of his fingers ached so badly that he had to soak them in ice water to keep the swelling down? It wasn't about the money, or getting a recording contract, or one day playing backup fiddle for a big time country and western star. No, it was about being recognized as the *best*. It was that desire that had brought him to this very night, to win this last in a series of contests.

To win, he knew he couldn't be just a little bit better than the other fiddlers. Each judge had his own way of ranking the contestants. One judge might not care for a tune a fiddler chose to play, or another judge might think the fiddler didn't smile the way he should, or that the audience didn't like him enough—or too much. It was never straightforward, so

Jason knew he had to be plenty better than everyone else, so much, so there could be no doubts. That was the goal.

The contest at last got underway. One fiddler after another, in order by the number drawn, stepped onto the stage and gave it his or her best. As Jason listened from the wings to each contestant his confidence grew. Number 9 was good—that was Bill Orland from Wisconsin—and number 12 was better still—a young woman from New Mexico who he had played against only once before. Good fiddlers most of them but not up to the mark when it came to beating him.

Then as contestant 15 launched into his second number, an odd feeling stole over Jason. Suddenly everything felt strange and out of control. He was hot, flushed, had a sour taste in his mouth. His stomach turned. Was he having a heart attack? He was too young for that. Maybe it was something he ate at the hotel, or he had a touch of the flu? There was still a contestant, number 16, before his turn came to play. He needed to get some air, so he pushed open the backstage door and stepped out onto the loading platform. He took a deep breath of the pine-scented mountain air and felt his head begin to clear. The queasiness left him and he rubbed his arms to regain his vitality. He had only a few minutes before his number was called. Cricket song filled the night; a summer half moon shone down on the cars and pickup trucks in the large parking lot behind the convention center. Jason found his thoughts stealing away to the days when he was a boy growing up in mountains. On such nights he would go raccoon hunting with his father or sit on the porch and play his fiddle to the whippoorwill and the other night creatures. The memories filled him with melancholy for something cherished but lost. He wanted to linger, but he knew he had to go back inside to compete. He could not allow his mind to be enchanted by the bittersweet phantoms of his youth.

He pulled the door open and went inside. He removed his fiddle from its case and checked the tuning, while going over in his mind the tunes he would perform: *Red Apple Rag* followed by *Lonesome Moonlight Waltz*.

But his concentration was arrested by the music he heard coming from the stage. Like a boxer stopped cold by a Sunday punch, his senses reeled. He knew that music; there could be no mistaking it. Only Ira Cockrill played a tune that way, with those odd shifts in tempo, and the notes, not pretty or fancy, splashing and gurgling like the clear water of Dutch Run during the spring thaw. Jason was listening to the sound of real old-time mountain fiddling, the kind of fiddling he seldom heard any more. He was both excited and puzzled. What in the world was the old man—he must in his eighties—doing playing in a fiddle contest way the heck out in Idaho? It was ten years or more since he visited his teacher. He meant to stop by lots of times, but something always seemed to come up with his work or he had to drive to a fiddle contest someplace. Oh, but it was good to hear the old tunes played that way again. It was like hearing them for the first time.

A wise woman once said, "Memories are gods." Along with the music, Jason also heard deep within the recesses of his mind the old man's voice talking about music being a gift and not something to lord over others. A fragile thing was fiddle music, an arrangement of momentary tones coaxed out a contraption made of the thinnest pieces of wood and held together with hide glue and strung with wire, weighing little more than a breath, an object that a child might crush under his foot as easily as breaking an egg. The violin, so like the human voice, laughing and calling people to dance or have a bit of fun, or reaching into the dark, sad places to help a person remember. One could draw from the well of life playing this kind of music, but there was the chance of destruction too, for the man with the hunger of pride in him.

These words came back to Jason, on the notes of the old man's music, and each, like a hammer stroke, chipping away the hard, brittle shell of selfishness and cupidity he had allowed to isolate his heart. He swayed as if suffering from vertigo, his breathing short and rapid. Then a bitter shame washed over him, so immediate and real, it felt as if acid was burning his skin: the hard words spoken to his wife, the lost friendships, the false kiss of the stranger, the hollow emptiness of his soul. How could he have strayed so far from the joys of life? Could he find his way back again?

Then the music was over, and he could hear the audience applauding. The familiar sound brought him back to himself. His face was wet with tears. He slipped the fiddle and bow back into the case and rubbed his eyes with his hands. He was the next contestant to play. Only he wasn't going to play. Not in this contest. Not in any contest. He had only one desire, to find his old teacher and thank him— thank Ira for everything.

He hurried onto the stage just as the old man exited the far side. He started to follow after him but was stopped by the master of ceremonies who grabbed him by the sleeve.

"Hold on there, fella," the man said cheerfully, addressing the audience as much as Jason. "Where are you off to in such a hurry? And where's your fiddle? You can't play for these good people if you don't have a fiddle."

Jason turned toward the waiting audience, but the bright stage lights rendered them invisible. He could, however, hear some of them chuckling. "I can't," he stammered. "I mean, I've got to find someone. It's important."

"You'll be disqualified if you miss your turn. You realize that, don't you?"

"I do. I don't want to be in this contest."

Jason freed himself from the MC who then turned to the audience. "Well, I guess there's a first time for everything. Must be some kind of emergency. But the show must go on. Would contestant 18 please join us now on stage." He looked down at his notes. "Our next contestant comes from Fresno, California, and her name is. . ."

Jason hunted backstage but couldn't find Ira. He went out into the parking lot, but there was no sign of the old man. Maybe he was staying at the hotel? Jason hurried to the hotel and searched the lobby, but without success. He asked the girl behind the registration counter to check if they had a Mr. Ira Cockrill staying in the hotel.

"Let me look," she said and flipped through the box of registration cards. "No, there's no one with that name staying with us."

"My name is Jason Walker. I'm staying in room 219. If Mr. Cockrill happens to check in, could you please tell him that I'm looking for him?"

"Jason Walker?" the girl said. "I have a message for you."

She handed him a slip of paper. The message was from his mother. It read:

"Ira Cockrill passed away earlier today. The funeral will be on Wednesday. I hope you can get back in time.

Love, Mom."

In less than an hour Jason was on the road. He made it back just in time for the funeral. He then set about trying to convince Julienne that he was a changed man. He continued to play the fiddle but he stopped going to contests, stopped staying out late and running after women. Gone was the pride and ambition.

Julienne had hired a lawyer without telling her husband, and the lawyer had begun drawing up divorce papers. But two months after Jason's return from Idaho, Julienne let the matter drop. If Jason continued doing his best to be a good husband and father, then she would look to the future, not the past.

And of all the days of the week, Saturday mornings were extra special for Jason Walker. That was when he gave lessons to the young people of the community who were drawn to fiddle music. He didn't teach them the fancy tunes he knew; he taught them the old-time tunes that Ira taught him. And he talked to the young people about music being a gift, a wonderful, magical gift, that becomes all the greater the more it is given away.

SHAVING A DEAD MAN

My father played the fiddle. When he died, my brother and I both wanted his violin. So we flipped a coin. I got the violin. My brother took home his cherished Winchester Model 94 deer rifle. The violin is not a valuable instrument as far as the world is concerned. I believe my father's Aunt Maddie purchased it from a Sears & Roebuck Catalog in 1906. She gave it to her favorite nephew after she was involved in a car accident and could no longer play. My father played the fiddle at family gatherings and with some of his work buddies who had a bluegrass band. Like the violin, my father's playing was average, but he loved making music and that is why having the instrument is important to me. It was a part of him.

I had no interest in learning to play the fiddle when I was young. I wanted to be a professional baseball player. Then I wanted to be a scuba diver, and after that someone who builds and flies hot air balloons. In the end, I became a lawyer. Alas, with such ease do we allow the dreams of our youth to slip away.

My saving grace, such as it is, is that I do not practice law in a big city, but in a small rural town and that keeps me relatively honest and interested in the people I represent. These include storeowners, insurance agents, schoolteachers, and farmers. The downside of my profession is that I spend so much of my time reading statutes, depositions, and case law, and that has a way of stifling the more imaginative and intuitive side of my nature. Therefore when a friend invited me to go to a music festival with him, I jumped at the chance. It wasn't, however, the kind of festival I expected, where bands performed on a big stage and everyone else sat in lawn chairs and listened. There was a small stage and people did sit in lawn chairs to listen to the performers, but the majority of the festivalgoers hung out in the campground or parking lot and played music. These impromptu jams were so full of vitality and a zest for life that I decided I wanted to be part of it all. When I got home I dragged out Dad's old fiddle but saw that it needed some work. For one, there were deep grooves in the fingerboard from my aunt and father pushing the strings down over so many years, and the tuning pegs were worn and tended to slip. So I took it to a luthier in town named Ben Carly.

Ben works the reference desk at our county library during the day and fixes musical instruments in the evenings and on the weekends. Behind his house he built a 12 ft. by 14 ft. building to use as his workshop. Everywhere you turn in the shop there are mandolins, guitars, fiddles, dulcimers, and banjos—even a couple of vintage Fender Stratocasters.

"Is it worth getting fixed?" I asked as Ben checked out the fiddle.

"Definitely. It wasn't an expensive instrument when it was new; it might have cost eight to twelve dollars back then, and that included the case and bow. But the German workshops before the wars turned out some fine student-grade instruments. My guess is this violin was made in Mittenwald."

He tuned the violin and bowed a tune, which brought back a rush of memories. He then tapped his knuckle along the edge of the instrument. He told me he was listening for places where the top was loose from the sides and needed to be reglued. Loose joints can cause a violin to buzz when it's being played.

Ben said he would start on the violin in a week, and I asked if I could come over and watch him while he did the work. It is fair to say that I am a creature of our modern age, always hurrying from one appointment or court date to another, checking my emails and returning phone calls. But after only a couple of minutes inside Ben's workshop, all I wanted to do was hang out and watch him perform his magic. Perhaps it was the aroma of aged wood and the tang of varnishes that acted upon me like some wizard's elixir, holding me fast in its spell. I am sure Ben was also a part of it. Not only could he fix instruments, he could spin interesting yarns as he did so. Like a friendly barber or old-fashioned politician, he had that rare ability to enchant the world with stories so that even the simplest events assumed mythic proportions.

I wound up spending a couple of evenings with Ben as he worked on my violin. He began with a steel scraper that he drew in long, steady strokes down the length of the ebony fingerboard, making a sound like an old woman sweeping a courtyard. Each pass removed little more than a dusting of wood, but Ben was in no hurry. As he worked, he talked. One of his favorite topics was the titles of fiddle tunes. Some titles commemorate important historical events: *The Eighth of January*, for instance, the day the Battle of New Orleans was fought, and *Booth Shot Lincoln*. Others evoke a strong image even before the first notes are played, titles such as *Swinging on a Gate, Dog in the Dishes*, and *Hell Among the Yearlings*.

Then as Ben employed emery paper to finish smoothing the fingerboard, he asked if I had ever heard a tune called *Shaving a Dead Man*. I tried to recall the names of the tunes my father played. *Red Wing* was one. I remembered it because it had words and he sang them sometimes, while he sawed the tune.

> *"There once was an Indian maid,*
> *A shy little prairie maid,*
> *Who sang all day a love song gay,*
> *As on the plains she'd while away the day.*
>
> *She loved a warrior bold,*
> *This shy little maid of old,*
> *But brave and gay he rode one day*
> *To battle far away.*
>
> *Now the moon shines tonight on pretty Red Wing,*
> *The breeze is sighing, the night bird's crying,*
> *For afar beneath the stars her brave lies sleeping,*
> *While Red Wing's weeping her heart away."*

Another tune he played was called *The Four-Poster Bed*, and at a certain point in the tune he would tap the top of the fiddle in four places with the end of his bow, a tap for each post of the bed. It always made people smile. I looked at the fiddle, and, sure enough, I could see little dents in the top where he tapped the fiddle. I mentioned this to Ben and he said he had already noted the dents and that the sheriff of Violin County should outlaw the playing of *The Four-Poster Bed*.

But I couldn't recall my father ever playing a tune called *Shaving a Dead Man*. Ben told me that whenever he thought of the tune it brought back a story he heard a long time ago, back when he first started working on instruments. I asked him to tell me the story and here it is, more or less, in his own words. I thought it was a good story and maybe you will, too.

Clarence Withrow was a farmer who lived up on Barklen's Ridge. He was funny old bird, an incessant worrier, who often worried things into happening. He also harbored a superstitious streak—two traits that often go together—so that if a black cat crossed his path on the way to town, he would turn right around and go home. If a bird flew into the house of a morning, he would take to his bed for the rest of the day to keep from having an accident. It was just the way he was and he had no more chance of changing it than a warthog has of winning a beauty contest.

And poor Clarence shared another trait with any number of small farmers who have weathered their share of hard times: he never threw anything away if there was the slightest chance he might find a use for it someday. That meant his barn, cellar, and sheds were crammed full of outdated farm implements, buckets of bolts, scraps of harness leather, and automobile transmissions.

To top it off, Clarence suffered from a rare neurological disorder. Every four or five years he would be going along just fine, when suddenly he would collapse and lose consciousness. To all appearances he was dead: no detectable heartbeat, pulse, or breath. He called these unusual blackouts his "sleeping spells." Some lasted only a couple of hours, while others might last an entire day. Once, when he was nine, he blacked out for three days and his parents were crazy with worry. Luckily, the doctor knew what it was and told them to be patient, and sure enough Clarence woke up feeling fresh as paint.

Now Clarence Withrow spent his adult life as a bachelor farming the two hundred and thirty acres he inherited from his father. But when Agnes Hackenmore, who lived on the adjoining farm, was widowed by the death of her third husband, James—he rolled his tractor trying to get the hay in before a thunderstorm hit—Clarence decided to try his hand at the courtship game.

A year and a month later the two were wed, but Clarence forgot to warn his new wife about his spells. Thus it came as quite a shock to the poor woman when one day, around three in the afternoon, she found Clarence laid out cold as a creek rock in the smokehouse, where he had gone to fetch a ham for that evening's supper. She should have called a doctor, but instead she called her brother, Luther, who hurried over to see what happened.

"It's just my blasted luck, Luther," she told her brother. "Seems like every man I marry up and dies on me. I swear I'm jinxed!"

"Now don't talk such foolishness, Agnes," Luther said. "These things just happen."

"But why does it always happen to me? I fear people will suspect I've had a hand in killing off my husbands."

"Now, now, nobody around here is going think that. You just have to tough it out and get on with your life. Are you sure he's dead?"

"Why, just look at him, Luther. Reckon I'll have to go see Bud Hartman and get him to make Clarence a coffin. Lord only knows, but I find this tedious."

So Agnes set about tackling a task she was only too familiar with. Bud Hartman ran the cabinet shop in town, but he also made coffins when the need arose. That included making three coffins for the Widow Odel/Nolan/Hackenmore in the past. Agnes came into his shop determined to get the very best for her most recent late husband.

"This time I want a natural wood coffin," she told Bud, "not a painted one. We came into this world without makeup and we should leave it the same way."

"I could make a simple pine coffin, if that's what you have in mind?" Bud said.

"Don't you have any wood that's got a pretty grain—walnut, maybe, or cherry?"

Bud showed her some walnut and cherry boards, but none of them quite suited her. He showed her some mahogany, but she turned that down, too. Then he pulled out three planks of the finest curly maple he said he had ever sawn.

"The best curly maple," Bud explained as Agnes ran the tips of her fingers over the grain of the wood, "comes from a tree that grows out by itself in a field or a clearing, not from a tree that grows back in middle of the woods."

"And why's that?" the widow asked.

"No one's exactly sure, but I believe it's because of the wind."

"What's the wind got to do with it?"

"Well, you see, a solitary tree moves back and forth in a strong wind a whole lot more than a tree jammed in among all the others. And all that swaying back and forth puts the curl into the grain somehow. Leastwise, that's my humble theory."

"It's as good a theory as any I can think of," Agnes agreed.

"And once I sand and finish the wood, the curl will pop right out," Bud added.

"This maple is exactly what I was looking for. When can you start to work? As warm as it is, I need to have the laying out and funeral as soon as possible."

"Aren't you going to hire an undertaker?"

"No, I have plenty of experience with this sort of thing. Best to keep it simple. Luther is digging the grave as we speak. I decided to plant Clarence up on the ridge next to the big sycamore he was so fond of."

She produced a slip of paper from her purse. "Here are his measurements. Luther did the measuring and I wrote 'em down."

She handed the paper to the carpenter.

"And one more thing," she said. "Could you carve my husband's initials into the top? And maybe a pair of birds perched on tree branches with leaves, too. Something to make it look extra pretty. Can you do that?"

This request did not surprise the cabinetmaker. He knew Agnes loved her gingerbread. She had gobs of it along the top of her porch and around the front windows.

"I'll get on it right away," he said. "Send Luther by first thing in the morning."

And that is how Clarence got his coffin. The only thing was, he wasn't dead. So the next day just about noon, with the house full of mourners all speaking in hushed voices and the "deceased" freshly-shaved and laid out straight and proper in his new funerary box, which had been set up on two sawhorses in the parlor, Clarence suddenly came to. He opened his eyes and sat upright, wondering what in blazes was going on.

Mrs. Allison in the front row was so startled she fainted dead away. So did Ned Butler standing in the back of the room. A great big lummox of a man, Ned reduced a small table to kindling as he collapsed, a feat that would take years for him to live down.

Of course, there were other assorted screams and oaths, but the person most upset by the whole affair was the guest of honor, Clarence Withrow.

"What in Sam Hill is going on?" he bellowed.

"We thought you were dead!" Luther said.

"But I ain't dead!"

"Oh, the saints be praised!" Agnes exclaimed, tears of gratitude welling up in her eyes. "Here, Clarence, let me help you out of the coffin."

That, however, turned into a more challenging ordeal than anyone expected. Clarence's arthritis was such that he had difficulty trying to lift his legs over the sides of the coffin, and when Agnes took an arm and tried to help him, it upset his balance and the coffin tipped over on its side. This caused one of the sawhorses to slide out from under the coffin and the box went crashing to the floor with Clarence spilling out and banging his head on the floor, his limbs all in a jumble.

More people jumped forward to help, hands grabbing at Clarence and lifting him to his feet, but his legs were wobbly from having been in his sleeping spell so long. He staggered to his favorite chair and sat down. He was also dehydrated, his throat dry as dust, so that his words came out as a series of croaks.

"Can someone get me a glass of water?"

Josey Winter, Agnes' second cousin, hurried into the kitchen to get the water while Clarence explained to Agnes about his spells. Two men lifted the coffin back onto the sawhorses and then they went out onto the porch to smoke. Mrs. Pryor sat in the corner and fanned herself with the fold-up fan she always carried in her purse, shaking her head in disbelief. At last, Pastor Harris managed to get everyone's attention and he led them in a prayer of thanksgiving.

Luther, meanwhile, was burdened with guilt. Just before he left, he handed Clarence a gold ELGIN pocket watch with the initials ℭ 𝔚 engraved on the case.

"I wasn't stealing it," he told Clarence sheepishly, "Agnes said I could have it."

In the days that followed, Agnes thanked her lucky stars that her fourth husband was still in the land of the living, and matters were soon back to normal, except that Clarence didn't know what to do with the coffin. Bud Hartman wouldn't take it back, nor could he be expected to, seeing as it was custom-built to order with Clarence's initials and a pair of wood thrushes carved into the top.

So Clarence hauled the coffin up into the attic and tried to forget the whole business. Only he couldn't. Waking up inside the coffin had rattled him good and, given the superstitious bent of his imagination, his memory of the event only grew more vivid in the days and weeks that followed. Night after night, he lay in bed staring up wide-eyed at the ceiling, picturing the accursed casket just above him among the hatboxes, trunks, and his grandmother's chifforobe. The vision kept him from falling asleep, and when he did at last fall asleep, it gave him nightmares.

At last he told his wife what was troubling him.

"If the coffin is ruining your peace of mind, just bust it up with the ax and burn it for firewood."

But this solution, sensible as it was, came up hard against the farmer's other quirk: he simply couldn't bring himself to throw anything useful away, no matter what it was.

The coffin had cost good money and he would just have to find some use for it. His first idea was to put it out in the barn next to the horse stalls and use it to store his currycombs, grooming brushes, and hoof picks. He later added his wood planes, hammers, and his prized HENRY DISSTON & SONS ten-point handsaw.

But that only worked for a couple of weeks, because the coffin, even though it was now a tool chest, and a highly decorative tool chest at that, still looked like a coffin, and every time Clarence went into the barn, which was dozens of times a day, he saw it and he got a sour taste in his mouth and the worry about dying would start up again.

He considered painting the inside of the coffin with pitch and putting it out in the lower pasture as a water trough for his livestock, but that meant he would see it every time we went to tend to his animals.

Then one afternoon, a neighbor named Ed Hanley stopped by to return some canning jars his wife had borrowed from Agnes. Clarence was fond of the younger man and he confided in him about his problem with the coffin. He even took Ed out to the barn and showed him his "agent of fear," as he called it.

"Ed, I know I'm being foolish, but that box is giving me the creeps."

Ed, as it happened, was a fiddler, and as he regarded the coffin he couldn't help but notice the quality of the wood used to build it. This gave him an idea.

"Clarence," he said once they were outside again and the coffin was hidden from view, "as I see it, your problem is that you've got something you don't want, can't use, but you're too tight to get shut of it."

The older farmer nodded his head like a man being told by his doctor that he has an incurable disease.

"I can feel it *waiting* on me, Ed, *waiting* for me to die good and proper, so we can go along together into the earth, like we were supposed to do in the first place. The accursed thing makes me feel like I'm living on borrowed time."

"It must have been a shock for you," Ed said.

"It was. And I sometimes think about waking up in that box after it was in the ground, clawing at the top and no way to get out."

Ed felt a shiver run through him and felt sorry for his friend.

"Then what you need to do is change its nature," said Ed.

"What are you talking about?"

"I use to own a black stallion called Major," Ed continued. "You remember him, a great big brute that did nothing but cause trouble. Had a mean streak a mile wide. I couldn't work him and I wouldn't sell him for fear he might kill the next guy. So I paid the vet to turn ol' Major into a gelding, and that settled him right down, turned him into the best horse I've ever owned. I could ride him, or throw a harness on him and he'd pull a plow, harrow, or rock sled all day. He was a great horse."

"But what's Major got to do with that dang box?"

"I know a violinmaker over in Dentonville. His name is Harvey Silks, and he would about kill for maple as pretty and curly as what's in that coffin of yours. I'll wager he could make four violins from that much wood, each with the finest back, sides, neck, and scroll you ever saw. So I'm thinking, you might do a trade with him."

"What kind of trade?"

"You give him the coffin for one of the fiddles he'd make out of it. That way, you'd get rid of the coffin and get something in return that you could really use."

"But I'm too old to start learning music."

"Nonsense. A person can take up music early or late. It's not like you've got your heart set on performing on the Grand Ole Opry. Fiddle playing is just a good way to unwind after working all day. And if you get tired of the violin, or your wife threatens to kick you out of the house because your playing is giving her a headache, then you can sell it for maybe more than you've got invested in the coffin. Why, I might even buy it myself."

"That's a first-class idea, Ed," Clarence said, a smile breaking upon his features as broad as sunrise, "that is just exactly what I'm going to do."

The next day Clarence drove his pickup over to Dentonville with the coffin in the back. Harvey was a decent violinmaker, even if he was self-taught, and he ran the palm of his right hand along the smooth sides of the maple coffin like a mother stroking her child's cheek. The deal was struck and four months later, Clarence had himself a lovely new fiddle. Ed Hanley gave him some lessons to help him get started and, as his younger neighbor had predicted, Clarence derived genuine enjoyment from playing the instrument each evening after supper as he slowly mastered the tunes he had listened to here and there all his life, tunes like *Bill Cheatham*, *Nancy Rowland*, and *Bull At the Wagon*—and even a tune called *Shaving a Dead Man*.

With the coffin gone, he also stopped worrying about being buried alive, gave up worrying about dying altogether. Which was a good thing, because he lived quite a few more years. When he finally did pass away—three doctors were brought in to make sure—he left his fiddle to Ed's youngest son, Roger, who wound up moving out to Wyoming to become a rancher. When Roger died, the fiddle went to his daughter who moved to San Francisco where she played it in a rock band.

Someone told Ben that she played backup fiddle for Bob Dylan and Taj Mahal, but he didn't think that was true. The rest of the story though, Ben assured me, happened just the way he said it did. He knew it was true because he heard the story from his cousin who heard it from his father-in-law, who used to live next door to. . .

DEVIL'S DREAM

Marcus Abernathy quit the Wells Fargo stagecoach a jumble of stiff joints and bruised muscles.

So this is Auburn, he thought as he stretched and surveyed the dusty boomtown, the oppressive heat making his throat dry. A freight wagon lumbered past, pulled by a pair of half-starved mules. Three men with heavy packs sprouting shovels and picks trudged by. One turned and gave Marcus a surly look as if to say, "We sure as Hades don't need another prospector in this lousy burg."

The driver's helper, a sallow-skinned scarecrow, flung back the oiled canvas flap that protected the coach's rear compartment from the elements and removed a soiled, stained carpet bag, which he flung on the ground at Marcus's feet as if it were filled with snakes.

"That be yours, I reckon."

Marcus grabbed the bag and sauntered up the street looking for a boarding house. All he owned in the world was a change of clothes, four cigars, a WADE AND BUTCHER razor with a bone handle, and a young man's bright dream of striking it rich in the gold fields of California.

"Try your luck up along the American River near the town of Auburn," the mate on the sidewheeler told him as they steamed their way east through the delta that lies between San Francisco and Sacramento, the blue water melding on both sides into a green sea of rippling grass. "Hangtown is another ripe town for gold, but too rough for my blood."

"Why's that?" Marcus asked.

"It's called Hangtown, ain't it? That should tell you all you need to know."

"Is it true what they say?" Marcus asked.

"Is what true?"

"That there are gold nuggets on the ground as big as hen's eggs just begging a man to pick 'em up."

The man barked a laugh, spat over the railing, and watched his spittle fall into the churned up water behind the paddlewheel before responding.

"Nothing's free in this life, sonny. Didn't your pappy ever teach you that?"

The crack made Marcus sore and he stomped over to the other side of the boat and stayed there for the remainder of the trip. Hosts of birds, large and small, soared and swooped over the verdant landscape, their cries drowned out by the fump, fump, fump of the steam engine as it punched balls of inky smoke into the sky from a pair of tall, black chimneys that straddled the wheel house.

Now, walking up the boardwalk in Auburn under a cloudless, cerulean sky, Marcus imagined he could hear the gold calling to him. Gold mining, he had made up his mind, was going to be a lark. A few months of moderately strenuous work and he would be set up for life. The first thing he would do with his fortune would be to build a mansion on top of a hill in San Francisco. He had seen one that caught his fancy when he passed through the city, an elegant structure with tall, stately windows, a rounded turret at one end, and a wrap-around porch. But his house, he decided, would be grander, and he would lounge on the porch all day drinking champagne as pretty women nodded to him as they passed by.

Marcus turned a corner and nearly bumped into a man with protruding teeth. "Watch where you're going, mister," the man snarled.

"You're the one best watch where he's going," Marcus shot back. He hadn't traveled five thousand miles and crossed the Isthmus of Panama to take guff from some bucktoothed idiot. He dropped his bag, spread his feet, and balled his fists. If the stranger wanted a brawl, why then Marcus Abernathy was just the banty rooster to give it to him.

The man instead pulled a bottle from of under his belt and tilted it up as he shuffled his way down the street.

Marcus chortled with satisfaction. He wasn't a man to be trifled with, not back in Philadelphia where his father was a minister of the Lord, nor here amongst these heathens. Yep, he aimed someday to be a *big* man in the West. Why, he might even get himself elected Governor. Anything was possible in California. It was a land brimming with possibilities.

Alas, Fate had other plans for Marcus Abernathy, and none of them good. For starters, Marcus spent the better part of that first summer so swollen with poison oak that his skin was left scarred in several places. The constant itching nearly drove him mad. His next misfortune was getting bit on his forearm by a rattlesnake. It happened while he was moving rocks, and he very nearly died—and often wished he had. Other calamities to befall him included busting his knuckle on a defective cradle, watching as his sluice box washed away in a flash flood, and having an ill-mannered mule step on his foot. It was while he was laid up from this last mishap that he took stock of his situation. He had mined for gold six ways from Sunday and had less than a hundred dollars to show for his troubles. What's more, he had grown to loathe the mining business and its endless back-aching, heartbreaking labor. His once smooth hands were now a rash of calluses, and his hair teemed with lice. There just had to be a better way of making a living. He considered opening a store, but he lacked the capital and the patience it took to put up with finicky customers and their whims. He tried to get a job in a saloon but lost out to another man who had bigger thumbs. He learned that the size of a man's thumbs mattered in California, because miners paid for most things, including shots of whiskey, with gold dust, and it was the bartender's prerogative to reach into the miner's poke and extract a pinch of the precious dust—the bigger the thumb, the greater the profit.

Marcus tried and failed at mule skinning, blacksmithing, and dealing faro. This last endeavor nearly cost him his life when a six-foot-five miner accused him of cheating. Marcus *was* cheating, but he had enough brains to deny it and got off with a sound thrashing.

Marcus even thought about going into preaching, like his father. It was plain to see that the citizens of Auburn were in sore need of moral instruction. In the end, however, given his fondness for liquor and women, Marcus had to abandon that idea as well.

Then one autumn evening in Auburn he entered a gambling tent and noticed a man playing the fiddle back next to the wood stove. The man was considerably older than most of the men in town, and he played with his fiddle resting on his chest rather than tucked under his chin. He wore a brushed frock coat with a velvet collar, polished black leather boots, and a felt hat with a white feather stuck in the band. Fascinated, Marcus stopped to listen, but could barely hear the melody over the roar of drunken voices, the staccato click, click, click of the wheel of fortune, the rattle of dice, and other assorted cries, coughs, and curses.

Marcus sidled up to the fiddler. "They give you money to play that thing?" he asked.

"I don't play for free," the man said as he finished up the tune. He bent down and retrieved the stogie he had left burning on the floor.

"What's your name?" Marcus asked. The man was cross-eyed and Marcus had trouble figuring out which eye to talk to.

"Cranshaw," the fiddler said. "What's yours?"

"Abernathy."

"Any kin to Sid Abernathy, the stage coach robber?"

"I come from righteous people," Marcus said stiffly. "My father is a minister of the Lord."

"I'm sorry to hear that," Cranshaw said. "Them Bible thumpers give me a sour stomach. All that preaching against the fiddle and folks having a good time."

He took a puff on his stogie, blew out a perfect smoke ring, and grinned with satisfaction.

Marcus decided to change the subject. "I like your music," he said. "Is the fiddle a hard instrument to learn how to play?"

"Depends,"

"Depends on what?"

"How much a body is willing to practice. And if he's got an ear for music."

"I got two ears like most folks."

"Yep, I can see you have," the man laughed. "But can you tell when a note sounds right? See, the fiddle is just like the human voice. There ain't no guides to help you like there is on the banjo. With the fiddle, you've got to open up your ears so you can hear the differences between the notes."

Marcus wanted to talk more but the gambling tent boss, a lobster-faced man named Fenmore, was glaring at Cranshaw and the fiddler knew it was time to get back to making music.

In the days that followed Marcus made a circuit of the other saloons and gambling tents in search other fiddlers, but didn't run into any. Which was Jim Dandy with him because that meant he could find work as a fiddler, provided he acquired a fiddle and the ability to play it.

One night he counted out Marcus money and judged he could survive for three months on what he had if he cut down on his drinking.

"That should be enough time to learn how to play. I'll just have to hunt up Cranshaw and get him to help me."

At closing time at the Gold Pan two nights later, Marcus made his proposition while Cranshaw was packing up his violin.

"I've made up my mind to become a fiddler just like you," he told the older man.

"That's nice," Cranshaw said as he tied a strip of cloth around his fiddle case to keep it from flopping open.

"But I've got to find me a fiddle first," Marcus whined.

"Yep, a fiddler needs a fiddle," Cranshaw said and then yawned. "Now, if you'll excuse me, I'm tired and need my bed."

"But I want to buy *your* fiddle. Here. I can give you twenty dollars."

Marcus held out a pair of ten dollar gold pieces.

The man looked at the coins and then at Marcus, his expression one of bewildered amusement.

"My violin is my livelihood, mister, so why in Pete's sake would I sell it to you?"

"But I need to get me a fiddle."

"I'll tell you what. There's a Chink that lends out money. They call him Harry Chan, but that's not his real name. Just ask around for him in China camp. I heard he took a violin in as security on a loan, but then the man who borrowed the money died from cholera. Old Harry might let it go cheap."

So Marcus acquired the fiddle from the Chinaman and set about learning how to play. Cranshaw showed him half a dozen simple tunes like *Liberty* and *Flop-Eared Mule*.

But God in his wisdom doesn't hand out musical talent willy-nilly and, try as he might, Marcus discovered he couldn't saw out a tune worth the effort.

One pull of the bow across the strings sent folks scurrying and one hard-luck miner even threatened to bust up Marcus' fiddle and make him eat it piece by piece if he didn't stop torturing the "poor creature."

So Marcus found an abandoned mine shack far from town and redoubled his efforts. By now winter had settled in and a heavy cold rain beat down on the roof of the cabin for days at a time. A field stone fireplace topped with a mud and stick chimney stood at one end of the cabin, and when Marcus wasn't fiddling he was cutting and hauling firewood in a vain attempt to stay warm. Most of his money was spent and he realized that it was either master the cursed instrument or starve.

The moon rose full one night as Marcus worked his way through the low part of *Sally Goodin* for the hundredth time. Even he could tell his fiddling sounded more like a mule braying down a mineshaft than music. At last his frustration reached its zenith and he stamped his foot and cried out, "The Devil take me, but I'll tame you or use you for firewood."

The words were no sooner out of his mouth than there was a sharp knock on the cabin door.

The sound so startled Marcus—he rarely got visitors—he nearly dropped the violin. He listened and the knock came again, louder this time. So he set down the instrument and grabbed his revolver. At the third knock, he pulled the hammer back and stepped toward the door. He eased it open just enough to spy who was outside. What he saw was an odd, roly-poly kind of fellow with piggish eyes and a bulbous nose. The man had a matted curtain of black hair that fell down to his shoulders from under a moth-eaten beaver top hat. He wore a black coat that was shiny at the elbows and pinched in the middle where it was buttoned over his potbelly. Marcus also noticed that the man held a violin case in his right hand, the leather covering scuffed in a dozen places.

The unexpected strangeness of the man's appearance stole away Marcus' powers of speech, and he inched the door open to have a better look.

"I understand your name is Abernathy," the stranger said in a nasally, grating voice.

"It might be," Marcus managed to get out. "But you ain't from around here, are you?"

"Who in tarnation is?" the man said pulling on his right ear.

"True enough," Marcus forced a laugh, "unless you're an Indian or Mexican."

"Ain't you going to invite me in?"

Marcus was about to say no when the thought flashed through his mind, this ain't no ordinary man. How many times as a child had he listened in rapture to his father's sermons?

"Oh beware that snake that tempted Eve in the Garden," his father would trumpet from the pulpit as the Holy Spirit descended upon him, his eyes ablaze, the sweat glistening on his forehead. "He is the accursed one who beguiled the lesser angels into rebelling and who was cast into the fiery lake by Michael, mightiest of archangels. He is the spawn of evil and his name is Lucifer, Satan, Beelzebub, Mammon, father of contention, founder of murder, tempter, and Prince of Darkness."

Marcus often had nightmares after listening to these exhortations. A red-skinned beast with horns, cloven hooves, and a pitchfork chased him through a blasted landscape as flames of everlasting torture licked at his heels, and he would wake up screaming, his bedclothes soaked with sweat.

But the pudgy man before him with the funny nose and ill-fitting coat couldn't be further from the dreaded fiend of fevered dreams. Where were his horns, unless they were hiding under that excuse for a hat? Nor could Marcus detect the stench of brimstone, and, instead of a pitchfork, the man carried a fiddle. All the same, Marcus knew with a dead certainty that the Enemy his father so often railed against was now standing on his doorstep. Only Marcus wasn't the least bit afraid.

"I know who you are," he said.

"I thought you might. You *did* call out for me."

"I did not," Marcus protested, but then he remembered his curse. "Well, I wasn't in earnest," he stammered.

The Devil shrugged. "Do you want me to leave, then?"

Marcus' mouth was dry and he was turned two ways at once. "What is this about? What do you want?" he demanded.

"Well, you see, Mr. Abernathy, I have something of a problem."

He looked at Marcus as if expecting Marcus to ask after his problem, but when Marcus didn't, he continued.

"I take no pleasure in insulting mortals, despite what some may say. Jehovah made mortals the way they are and, as we all know, His workmanship can be shoddy at times. In your case, Mr. Abernathy, I must be blunt: your fiddling is an abomination. Even my imps and demons are complaining. So I decided to pay you a visit and offer you my services."

"What kind of services?"

"Yes, well, don't you think we'd be more comfortable discussing this indoors? I've come a long way and I wouldn't say no to a taste of whiskey and the warmth of your fire."

Marcus felt his guard go up. Not because he was talking to the Devil, but because his whiskey bottle was only a third full, and he wasn't keen to share it with anyone, least of all with such a shabbily-clad denizen of the underworld. And yet, he was bound by the law of hospitality, so he stepped back and motioned for the Devil to enter the cabin.

The Devil went to the fire and set the fiddle case on the floor. He removed his coat and shook the rain from it. He then rubbed his chubby pink hands together and rocked back and forth on his heels, the firelight dancing upon his fat, satisfied face.

"Mighty foul weather you have here in this part of the world. I don't take kindly to getting chilled, but I do benefit from the exercise."

Scratching his scalp up under his hat, which made the right side of his face squint, the Devil turned and looked at Marcus and Marcus noticed that he was missing several teeth. A sorry-looking customer, Marcus thought, as he poured a finger of whiskey into a glass and passed it over. It never occurred to him that the Lord of Heaven would condemn his former angel to such reduced circumstances. Or maybe it was just a clever ruse by the Devil to disarm his prey by appearing ridiculous. Marcus was tempted to ask him, but what could he hope to learn from the Father of Lies.

"Do you have a name?" Marcus said.

The man laughed. "Bunches of 'em, but Scratch will do for now."

"Well, Mr. Scratch, tell me about this service you have to offer."

"Why, I'm here to give you music lessons, Mr. Abernathy. I taught many of the great violinists of this world. The Italian Arcangelo Corelli, the grandfather of all gifted violinists was my pupil, as was Nicolo Paganini, a virtuoso of the first order. His name comes from the word "pagan," did you know that? And then there was the Frenchman, Pierre Gavinies. How the ladies admired his playing— But I see that I am boring you. Here then, let me show you what I mean."

He threw back the whiskey and tossed the cup to Marcus, who had to jump to catch it. The Devil then opened his case and withdrew a violin. The wood was stained blood red and in place of the scroll was a carved head of a horned he-goat with its tongue sticking out. The Devil reached down and pulled out a bow and placed the instrument under his chin, winked at Marcus, and began to play.

Never in his life had Marcus heard such a sound. The notes flew into the air like sparks from a smithy's hammer, startled like the mad rattling of summer hail upon a slate roof, excited like a bee hive getting ready to swarm. The melody as it danced and dipped and soared made Marcus' hair stand on end and his brain swim with giddiness. There was little in the music that was sweet, yet it was as seductive as Chinese opium with a kick like raw whiskey doctored with gunpowder. It awoke in Marcus an overwhelming desire, a desire for more. More of everything. More money. More women. More fighting. And yes, more devilment.

With each variation of the tune, Marcus beheld a vision: the gleaming battlements of a mountaintop castle, its walls and towers white as bone under a night sky slashed by shooting stars, a satyr cavorting with nymphs in a grove of ancient willows, a giant snake with golden skin coiled around an egg as large as a ship upon the sea. The egg began to crack—

"Well enough of that," the Devil broke in, ceasing the tune in mid-phrase and lowering the fiddle from his chin. "Don't suppose I could have another splash of that whiskey?"

Marcus opened his eyes and blinked, awakened from his trance. The cabin felt cold and empty; the fire had been reduced to exhausted embers. How long had Mr. Scratch played his fiddle? There was no way to tell. The music had suspended earthly time.

Woodenly, Marcus poured the last of the whiskey into a cup as the Devil wiped the rosin from his fiddle with a red silk handkerchief, which he then used to blow his nose.

"Thank you," he said, taking the cup from Marcus and draining it with one gulp. "Fiddling's thirsty work." He wiped his lips with the back on his hand. "Well, what do you think? Haven't lost the old touch, have I?"

"I'd give anything to play like that," Marcus exclaimed. He still felt the music coursing and vibrating through every sinew in his body. He trembled.

"Ah, but do you mean that, Mr. Abernathy?" the Devil studied him. "Would you truly give *anything?*"

"I do. I mean, yes, I would. Just name your price, Mr. Scratch."

"Let me see that fiddle of yours," the Devil said holding out his hand.

Marcus grabbed his fiddle from the table and handed it over to the Devil, who held it up to his ear and plucked the strings, one after another, from the lowest to the highest. G - D - A - E. He then brought the fiddle up close to his eyes like a nearsighted man reading a newspaper and examined the instrument from scroll to tail piece. He flipped it over and studied the back, tapping the maple here and there with a cracked, yellow fingernail.

At last he handed the fiddle back to Marcus. "You have a decent enough violin and I'll teach you how to play it. But don't ever sell it or trade it for another. This one must suit you for the rest of your days."

Marcus was confused.

"Why can't I sell or trade my fiddle?"

The Devil shook his head. "That would be a wrong and stupid thing to do, Mr. Abernathy."

"Why?"

"Because every fiddle that's ever been made has its own unique tone, just as you can tell one person's voice from another, even in the dark. And every fiddler has his own style of playing the violin. Some play fast, some slow. Some stress the down-bow, others the up-bow. Tone and style. They go together like a signature. One of a kind."

He looked into the empty cup and then at the depleted whiskey bottle and sighed.

"So you see, Mr. Abernathy, should I ever hear that fiddle played by someone else, even a single note, then I'll know you've finished with it, and with your life as well. That's how the contract works. I teach you to play, and in exchange I get your soul when you've lived out your allotted time on this Earth."

This was the first time the words "contract" and "soul" had been uttered, but Marcus already knew that they were the gist of any bargain with the Devil. His father banged on day and night about the immortal soul like one of them infernal rainmakers beating his drum, until Marcus couldn't stand it. What was the old man talking about? Marcus had never seen a soul. He had never touched, tasted, smelled, or heard one cry out. So if souls *did* exist, he reasoned, then they couldn't be all *that* important. He didn't know one miner who gave a hoot about his soul. All they talked and dreamt about was gold.

"Can you tell me how long I have to live, Mr. Scratch?" Marcus asked.

The question appeared to pain the Devil. "I can't rightly say. Not my line, if you see what I mean." He jerked his thumb up toward the ceiling. "You could live for years or be dead tomorrow. What *I* want doesn't enter into it."

Marcus found himself weighing the cost against the benefits. He was at the end of his rope and knew it, dead broke and no way to earn two bits as far as he could tell. He had always gone West when life turned dodgy, but now he had come to the limit of the West. Beyond stretched only the vastness of the deep blue Pacific. Nor could he return home, not after the way he cursed his father the night he left. So it was either drink mercury and die, or go crazy like the failed miners he saw hanging around town who were forever talking to themselves and emptying spittoons for the promise of a drink.

"Mr. Scratch, I reckon we have ourselves a deal. Let's shake on it."

The Devil smiled, his puffy cheeks glistening with sweat. He wiped his hand on the front of his coat and extended it to Marcus.

"Well then," the Devil said after the shake, "I reckon it's time we begin your first lesson."

A month later Marcus moved back to town. The first thing he did was go see Giles Mitchum, who owned a popular saloon in Auburn called the Gold Pan with his partner "Crazy" Janey. Both Giles and Janey guffawed when Marcus claimed that he could out fiddle anyone in California.

"I'll just have to show you then, won't I?" Marcus said. He whipped out his fiddle and launched into a tune before the startled partners could stop him.

He played *Forked Deer* fast enough to burn the hair off a six-point buck and then switched keys and tore through *Fire on the Mountain* till both Giles and Janey had to run to the door to make sure a wall of flames wasn't roaring its way into town from out of the American River canyon.

"Mister, that's the best dang fiddling I ever heard," Giles stammered. "It's got a heap of power in it and sure gets the heart thumping."

Giles turned to Janey who nodded in agreement.

"We'll pay you to play every night of the week, if you've a mind," she said. "Of course, you can take Sundays off if you want."

"Why would I want to do that?" Marcus asked.

"Well, some folks think it ain't right to play fiddle music on the Sabbath."

"Hang the Sabbath," Marcus snorted. "If you're open, I'll play."

After some spirited wrangling, a wage was settled upon and Giles and Marcus shook hands to bind the deal.

That night Marcus showed off his newly acquired musical talent to the saloon's patrons. And boys, didn't they have themselves a genuine gold rush fandango. Some of the men even tied red kerchiefs around their arms to mark that they were dancing the ladies' part, and the impromptu reels and squares lasted far into the night.

Word quickly spread through the surrounding mining camps that something altogether new was to be found in Auburn town, and a man would be a fool not to go and have a listen.

As a matter of fact, the winter rains had so raised the rivers that it was impossible to do any mining, and the town was teeming with out-of-work forty-niners. A combustible mixture of gold dust, alcohol, and frustration led to dozens of fights, and not a few deaths. As far as Marcus was concerned, this only added to the entertainment. He fiddled a breakdown every time some out-of-luck miner lunged across a card table with his Bowie knife to gut the dealer. Sometimes Marcus had to duck to keep from getting beaned by a flying whiskey bottle, but he kept right on playing. Yep, there was no doubt about it. Marcus Abernathy had found his vocation in life.

Now and again Marcus took a break from fiddling at the Gold Pan so he could visit some of the other gold camps.

He would start out in Oroville and work his way south through Angel's Camp and Sonora until he reached Mariposa. Then he would turn around and come back the other way. Everywhere he went miners flocked to hear him play his fiddle. There was something in his playing that stirred the hearts of these coarse-grained men, so far from home and loved ones. The music made them sad and happy at the same time, and they showed their gratitude by filling Marcus' pouch with yellow dust and his ears with compliments. He took to smoking Cuban cigars, swigging bonded spirits, and ordering only the best cuts of steak. No slaving underground breathing deadly rock dust or humping barrels of salted pork from wagon to store for Marcus Abernathy. And even though he wasn't rich, if things kept on the way they were going, he soon would be. Then he would build that mansion on a hill in San Francisco and live out his remaining years in style and comfort. He seldom thought about Mr. Scratch—the whole affair in the mountain cabin seemed like a far-away dream rather than something that really happened—and Mr. Scratch was such a funny looking man; it was nigh on impossible to take any of it seriously.

And yet, Marcus did sometimes have nightmares from which he awoke in a sweat, shaking with dread. Then the truth of his situation would press in upon him. He had pledged away his eternal soul, and that ill-considered, hastily given pledge troubled his conscience. Then Marcus would take a swallow of whiskey and shout into the darkness, "When you're dead, you're dead, so why fret about it?" That helped steady his nerves so he could fall back asleep again.

Then the gold in California began to peter out, and many of the miners drifted east to Nevada, where rich seams of gold and silver had been discovered. They called this strike the Comstock Lode, and Marcus began to lay plans to cross the Sierras and try his luck in Nevada for a spell.

But he never made it. One moonless Saturday night in Auburn, as he stepped out of the Gold Pan onto the boardwalk, reeling a bit from drink, a rifle bullet tore through the right side of his chest. The force of the impact spun him around like a dervish and he fell and landed face down in the muddy street. A miner a dozen yards away saw what happened and came running, but he was too late. Marcus never regained consciousness, his life's blood seeping out of the wound to mingle with the mud and other filth of the street.

The identity of the shooter was never discovered. Some believed, the sheriff included, that Marcus' death was a case of mistaken identity; someone out to settle a score shot Marcus in the dark by mistake. Bushwhacking of that sort was known to happen in the gold fields back then.

Others, however, believed that Marcus was killed on purpose, that he had argued with a gambler named Sloan over a woman, and Sloan had pulled the trigger.

Whatever the reason for Marcus' untimely demise, the shopkeeper J.P. Longwell (who doubled as a mortician when needed) agreed to lay Marcus out in the front room of his store. The burial was set for Monday.

And here is the sad part: despite his popularity as a musician, Marcus didn't have what you might call true friends, so no one mourned his passing. There was a man, however, who lived in a nearby camp who had heard about the shooting and decided to pay his respects. His name was Sandy Parker and he hailed from Tennessee. He was also a fair-to-middling fiddler and he hoped he might find a way to take possession of Marcus' violin; the neck had come loose from his own fiddle and he didn't know anyone who could fix it.

The journey to Auburn took longer than Sandy expected, and he didn't arrive in town until just past eleven o'clock on Sunday night. He banged on the door of Longwell's store until he woke the proprietor.

"What in heaven's name do you want at this hour of the night?" Longwell growled when he opened the door, an oil lamp in one hand and a pistol in the other.

"I've come to pay my respects to the deceased," Sandy said.

"Are you kin?"

"No."

"A friend?"

"An acquaintance. I saw him fiddle a couple of times. He sure could make that box sing."

"I don't care for music," Longwell said, "a big waste of time." The storeowner lowered his pistol and pushed the door open. "Well, you better come in."

Sandy stepped into the small shop. Oak barrels lined one wall and stocked shelves with coils of rope and gold pans lined another. In the center of the room was a table with a naked pine coffin sitting on top.

"Not much to see," Longwell said, laying the pistol down and turning up the wick of the lamp to illuminate the scene. "I already nailed shut the coffin for tomorrow's burying."

"Say, do you know what happened to Abernathy's fiddle? Did someone come and fetch it?"

"Well, that's the strange part of it," The shopkeeper scratched his chin. "The sheriff found a handwritten note tucked inside Abernathy's money belt. It was worn and soiled, but the note said that, no matter what, when his time came he was to be buried with his violin. The note also said that no one should play the violin under any circumstances. They should just put it in the coffin."

"The note said *that?*"

Longwell nodded his head. "It was his last wish so that's what I did."

"It seems an awful shame to let a good violin like his go to ruin."

"Well, like I said, I'm not much for music."

They stood looking at the coffin without speaking, each mulling over his own dark thoughts.

"Well, it's high time I was back in bed," Longwell broke the spell. "Tomorrow's a full day."

Sandy wasn't sure what to do. He had no place to stay, it was late, and he didn't know the town.

Longwell sensed the younger man's indecision.

"Where I grew up back East, someone always sat up with the dead. You seem an honest sort. If you want to sit up with the corpse, you're welcome to. I'll leave you the light."

The storekeeper placed the lamp on the counter, picked up his pistol, and slipped through a doorway into the back room where he had his bed.

Sandy pulled a chair up next to the coffin and sat down. His feet hurt from walking. Sandy first heard Marcus play nine months earlier, and he admired the fiddler's skill and power. He had heard Marcus play three times since then. When Sandy was growing up in eastern Tennessee, he had met lots of fellows who could saw out a tune or two on the fiddle, but none of them could touch Marcus. He was in a class by himself.

Sandy yawned and stretched. He was tired but not sleepy. Looking at the closed-up coffin, he called upon his King

James and the Book of Job: "Man that is born of a woman is of few days, and full of trouble."

And as he uttered these words a weird sensation crept over him, a restless concoction of curiosity and desire.

Had Longwell really put the fiddle in the coffin? He could have just as easily hidden the instrument, so he could sell it the next time he visited Sacramento or San Francisco. Having taken the measure of the storekeeper, however, Sandy had a difficult time convincing himself of this.

That got him wondering. How had Longwell positioned the fiddle inside the box? Did he place it on the dead man's chest with the hands folded over it? That is how testaments were buried with people, reading material for the journey to heaven. Only Sandy, given the rumors he had heard, didn't think Marcus was bound for that great celestial city. So he sat and pondered the question of the violin for several long minutes. Perhaps Longwell had snugged the fiddle in next to Marcus' side. But which side? Next to his bowing arm would be the best choice.

The lamp began to sputter, making the shadows on the wall dance; Longwell snored in the back room, fast asleep.

"I've just got to know if the fiddle is in the coffin or not," Sandy whispered to himself. "It won't hurt none to just take a little peek."

But another inner voice held him back.

"It doesn't do to trouble the dead. Marcus willed the fiddle buried with him and that's all there is to it."

The first voice returned with its rebuttal.

"The poor sod is shut of this world and can't use that fiddle where he's going."

"So you mean to steal it? Better to grab your hat and go home."

"I'll not go home, and it's not stealing. I'd just be putting that fiddle to good use where otherwise it would just rot."

Slowly, the part of him that wanted nothing to do with peeking inside coffins fell silent, argued down by the part that lusted after the violin.

And soon the desire grew into action. Sandy reached down and removed the hunting knife he kept tucked in his boot. He pushed the tip of the blade into the crack between the side of the coffin and the lid and worked the blade up and down until the nails began to loosen, taking care not to make too much noise. He was sweating, but he couldn't tell if this was from the effort of prying open the coffin, or fear at what he might find when he did. Even if he wanted to stop, he couldn't. Some external power had gained mastery over his will and was now animating his muscles.

The night was still when he arrived, but he now heard the wind kicking up. It came in gusts, whistling as it blew under the eaves. Longwell's snoring stopped and Sandy's knife hand froze as he listened to the storekeeper turn over with a grunt. In a half a minute, Longwell was snoring again.

A few more twists of the knife and the nails came free, and Sandy gingerly lifted the lid and laid it on the floor. The violin gleamed in the lamplight, proud and lonesome upon the dead man's chest with the bow resting beside it. Sandy reached out and picked them up, taking pains not to look at Marcus' frozen, pallid features.

With the fiddle now on his lap, he stroked the wood as he would a kitten. Whatever power had taken hold of him grew even stronger. All the same, he feared waking the storekeeper, so he thumbed the D every so gently. Just once. A single note. As quiet as a baby's sigh. But the sound of the note grew, and grew, and grew until Sandy, terrified, let go on the fiddle and clapped his hands over his ears. More notes, a torrent of notes, now ran together to compose a frantic melody. Sandy could see the violin strings shimmering as they vibrated. The lamp sputtered again and the wind buffeted the windows and moaned. With his right hand Sandy grabbed the neck of the instrument hoping to deaden the strings. But the haunting music would not be stilled. Not knowing what else to do, he jogged the fiddle into the coffin on top of the dead man. The moment he did this, the coffin began to dance, one corner banging the table followed by the next to the tempo of the tune. BANG, BANG, BANG, BANG, the coffin beat time, making Sandy's teeth grind and the hair on the back of his neck stand on end.

Then, without warning, there was a tremendous EXPLOSION! The force lifted Sandy backward out of his chair and flung him into a row of barrels, his head striking one of the metal bands that secured the oak staves. Dazed from the blow, he watched as a fountain of red and orange flame shot up into the air from inside the coffin. Then a cascade of debris rained down on him and he scrambled under the table for cover. Smoke and dust hung in the air, making Sandy cough. His head throbbed, his mouth filled with the foul taste of sulfur. He tried to remember the words to the Lord's Prayer. "Our Father, who art in heaven. . ."

A hand was on his shoulder, shaking him. He opened his eyes—he must have passed out—and there was a light. Two men loomed over him. One held a lantern while the other, J.P. Longwell, shook him. Sandy could see the storekeeper's lips moving, but he couldn't hear his voice. The memory of the explosion and fireworks came back to him, and he realized the explosion had deafened him.

A third man appeared and helped Longwell pull Sandy out from under the table. As they did, Sandy looked up and saw stars twinkling through a jagged hole in the roof. All about him were splintered boards and shards of roof shakes.

Meanwhile, the man holding the lantern moved over to the coffin, now motionless on top of the table.

"Great God Almighty," he exclaimed, "he's gone!"

"What are you talking about?" Longwell said.

"He's gone, J.P. Look!"

The man tilted the coffin on its side and Longwell and Sandy saw that the body was indeed gone and the inside of the coffin was charred black.

"What are you playing at, mister?" Longwell demanded, glaring at Sandy.

Although Sandy couldn't hear the storekeeper's words, he knew their meaning from the anger and fear evident in the storekeeper's eyes.

"It weren't me. I swear—"

He rubbed his ears; it was strange not hearing his own words.

"Get him out of here," Longwell said, and the other man guided Sandy outside. The night air smelled sweet after the foulness inside the store.

Sandy brushed the dust from his clothes and his hair with the clumsy motions of a drunk. His hearing was beginning to return, and he could faintly hear the voices of the men who gathering outside the store. Soon there was a sizable crowd and Longwell appeared to bar the door to the store.

Despite a blizzard of shouted questions, Longwell refused to say more than, "There's been an accident. Nobody's hurt. Now go home."

The sheriff appeared, pushing his way through the crowd. He conversed with Longwell for several minutes while everyone stood and waited.

The sheriff then took a lantern and went inside. He returned in a few moments and told everyone to go home.

This time the men obeyed, ambling off in twos and threes, exchanging theories about what had caused the explosion.

Before Sandy could leave, however, the sheriff took him by the arm.

"You best give me your side of the story, mister," he said.

"I don't have a side," Sandy said. His throat felt like it was full of ground glass, and talking was painful. "I was sitting there next to the coffin when it blew up." He decided it was best not to mention how he had pried the coffin lid off with his knife.

"Do you know where the body is?" the sheriff asked.

"No."

The lawman studied Sandy for a long moment, then shrugged. "Well, I reckon you're free to go, but I might want to talk to you later. Where can I find you?"

Sandy told him where his camp was located, and the sheriff re-entered the store with Longwell. Sandy started up the street. He wondered if the violin had survived the explosion. There was so much debris, it would take some searching to find it, but he was so badly shaken, all he wanted to do was go home.

"The Devil keep that fiddle," he muttered as he hoofed it along the southbound road out of town.

The stories that made their way through the towns and mining camps of the northern Sierra in the days and weeks following the incident were as inventive, varied, and seductive as any told by Scheherazade. The theory with the greatest currency held that it was an elaborate con orchestrated by Marcus Abernathy, with Longwell as his accessory, to outwit some card sharks who were pressing the fiddler to make good on his gambling debts.

"Relative of mine swears he saw Abernathy two weeks ago sashaying down C Street in Virginia City, big as life," claimed a blacksmith in Grass Valley, enthralling a group of miners waiting to get their shovels and picks sharpened. "It was all a set-up. No corpse went missin', see, because Marcus Abernathy never *died* in the first place. Longwell was in on it. Abernathy paid him to put a charge of gunpowder in the coffin and blow it up."

"But the coffin weren't blown up," Al McIlhenney objected. "It was just burned out, like how some Indians burn out a log to make a canoe. They set a fire so it burns real slow and—"

"Damn it, Mac, you don't know what you're talking about," the blacksmith spit. "The explosion nearly brought down the place. The way I've got it figured is that Longwell's no miner, and he didn't know how big a charge to use. Why, he nearly killed that poor fellow, the one sitting up with the corpse."

"And that's another thing," Mac said, determined to nail the faked death story to the counter. "Who was that man? What was he doing there? Was he kin to Abernathy? He sure lit out in a hurry. It's darn suspicious, if you ask me."

The men nodded their heads. There was real trickery in what had happened, and no mistake.

Yet, as each man took his tools and started back to camp, he entertained another explanation within the snug privacy of his own mind, an explanation he was afraid to give voice to lest it be true. The explanation was this:

Marcus Abernathy was a desperate man, and that desperation drove him to make a bargain with the Devil. That is how he got to play the fiddle with such skill. One day everyone was for running him and his accursed fiddle out of town; the next, they couldn't get enough of his playing. No one can learn music that fast without the supernatural playing a hand. The clue to the Auburn mystery centered on the note that Marcus wrote, ordering that his fiddle be buried with him. Why would he write such a note? Was he trying to outwit the Devil in some way? Well, if that was his dodge, he *was* a fool. A promise made is a debt unpaid, as the old-timers say, and the Devil is always watching. Watching and waiting. Waiting and listening. And he will be there when the time comes. You can count on it. He knows what is owed him, and he will collect on it, too.

ACKNOWLEDGMENTS

I wish to thank Carol Piening, John Blasius, Robert Ray, Kevin Burke, Anna McHugh, Paula McHugh, Mary W. Ybarra, and the lovely souls at First Christian Church in Olympia, Washington, for their generous help with this book. I also want to thank the many fiddlers, banjo players, and other musicians and storytellers who have inspired me over the years, and in particular the elders who helped me discover the source of the deep magic. These include Glenn Smith, J.P. Fraley, Melvin Wine, Lynn Springsten, Frank and Jane George, Wilson Douglas, Sherman Hammons, Lester McCumbers, Ira Mullins, Lee Triplett, Oleta Singleton, Betty Farmer, Lee Sexton, and Donald Riddell. I also owe a debt of gratitude to Joe Dobbs, Dwight Diller, Craig Johnson, Dave, Mike, and Tim Bing, Forrest Newton, Utah Phillips, Freyda Epstein, and Laurie Lewis.

ABOUT THE AUTHOR

Joe McHugh is a storyteller, writer, public radio journalist, and homegrown philosopher. In 1970, he purchased an eighty-acre farm in Gilmer County, West Virginia, where he raised goats, chickens, and draft horses. He also fell in love with the traditional music and storytelling of the southern Appalachian mountains. He performs with his wife Paula Blasius-McHugh, a musician and artist whose painting are inspired by the titles of American and Celtic fiddle tunes.

To learn more about their work, please visit:
www.americanfamilystories.org
www.joemchugh.info

Books by Joe McHugh
www.callingcrane.com

Slaying the Gorgon:
The Rise of the Storytelling Industrial Complex

Kilowatt
A novel about the energy industry, global warming, and our troubled relationship with time.

Flying Santa:
A True Story

Ruff Tales:
High Octane Stories from the Ruff Creek General Store

Better Than Money:
Tales to Treasure for a Lifetime

Made in the USA
Charleston, SC
23 February 2015